LEAVE OVER

Maternity leave over, DI Casey Clunes is straight back in the thick of it on her return to Brockhaven CID — an unidentified body washed up at Keeper's Cove, a possible arson attack at a nearby amusement arcade and an assault and robbery at a local convenience store . . . And in *A Tough Workout*, joining the local gym benefits Casey's crime-solving along with her fitness levels, as she gets the inside track on a string of local burglaries.

GERALDINE RYAN

LEAVE OVER

Complete and Unabridged

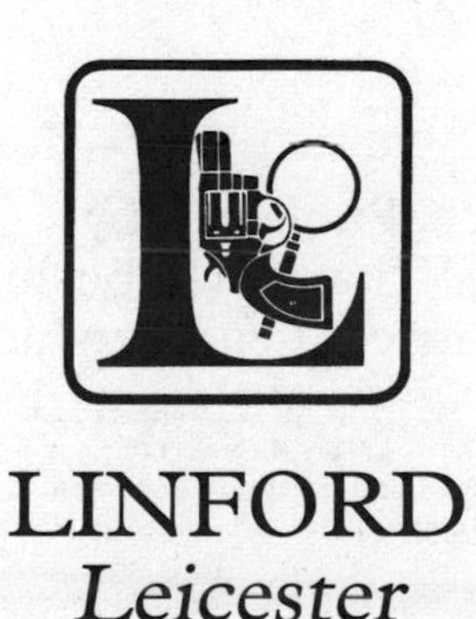

LINFORD
Leicester

First published in Great Britain

First Linford Edition
published 2012

British Library CIP Data

Ryan, Geraldine, *1951 –*
Leave over.- -(Linford mystery library)
1. Detective and mystery stories.
2. Large type books.
I. Title II. Series
823.9′2–dc23

ISBN 978–1–4448–0999–2

Published by
F. A. Thorpe (Publishing)
Anstey, Leicestershire

Set by Words & Graphics Ltd.
Anstey, Leicestershire
Printed and bound in Great Britain by
T. J. International Ltd., Padstow, Cornwall

This book is printed on acid-free paper

Leave Over

'What a day to go back to work!'

Casey had been encouraging Finlay to feed himself for some time now.

'I don't want one of those sons who rely on their mothers for everything to the extent that they're still living at home when they're thirty.' She'd been adamant about this.

'Casey, he's nine months old,' her long-suffering partner, Dom, had sighed. 'Cut the boy a bit of slack!'

'I cut him plenty,' she'd replied. 'It's just that with you males it's never too early to start training you up. I see it as my duty to his future life partner to raise a male child who refuses to be daunted by the combination of a washing machine and an overflowing laundry basket.'

Actually, Finlay was doing very well. Most of his porridge had landed in or near the vicinity of his adorable little mouth. Between mouthfuls he waved his bright green plastic spoon like a baton, in time to the music blaring from the radio.

'This is Brockhaven FM. Your first choice for local radio. And as we head for 7.30 let's go over to the news desk for an update.'

In five minutes, Debbie, the nanny Dom and Casey had selected from what had originally felt like a cast of thousands, would pull up outside in her cheerful yellow mini and take over. Thankfully she shared Casey's approach to independent feeding.

'A man's body has been washed up at Keeper's Cove. So far the body remains unidentified,' the newsreader announced. 'A fire at an amusement arcade in Brockhaven has caused extensive damage. Police speculation as to the cause of the fire does not rule out arson.

'A local shopkeeper is in hospital after an attack on the convenience store he runs, one of two branches of Bandali and Son, in Brockhaven. Police say that Mr Bandali Senior attempted to thwart a robbery at his store round about nine thirty last night and received several blows to the head and body. Thieves got away with the contents of the till. And now the weather . . . '

A car horn alerted Casey of Debbie's arrival.

'What a day to go back to work after maternity leave, eh?'

Debbie gave the impression of being older than her twenty-five years, which Casey put down to those comfortable shoes and no nonsense manner. She was a bit like a younger version of Julie Andrews, in Mary Poppins, minus the hat and brolly, Casey and Dom both agreed. Just what they wanted. She bustled in and swooped down to kiss the top of Finlay's head.

'Good morning, Finlay Clunes-Talbot,' she said. 'And how are we today?'

A gurgling Finlay generously offered her a spoonful of porridge. Debbie had already spent the odd few days with him on a 'practice run' as she called it and nanny and charge were already firm friends.

'Yum, yum,' she said, skilfully avoiding actually eating any of it, without hurting Finlay's feelings.

Casey slipped on her coat. Today she was back at work full-time after being at home on maternity leave for so long. This was no practice run but the start of their new routine. She was going to have to do this quickly and without a backward glance. Not because her departure would upset Finlay, who was by now fully engrossed in Debbie's company, but because she knew how much she'd miss him once she left.

If that wasn't bad enough she couldn't help feeling apprehensive at the prospect of returning to work. She'd been away a year. People would have come and gone. Systems may have changed. Although she'd been at Brockhaven nick for what seemed a lifetime, this morning she felt like the new girl.

'Right then,' she said, taking a deep breath. 'I'd better go and solve all those crimes.'

'Make sure you do,' said Debbie over her shoulder, as she cheerfully applied a flannel to Finlay's sticky hands and face. 'Just wave bye-bye and be off. It'll be all right, you know. Trust me.'

So she hadn't fooled Debbie in the slightest with her confident parting shot, then. She was a clever girl, that one. Hiring her had definitely been the right choice.

* * *

Stepping inside the building of the Brockhaven and District Police Constabulary was a bit like revisiting your family home after you'd moved out. Her emotions alternated every few seconds. The familiarity of the same office layout and many of the usual familiar faces were comforting.

But then she'd spot someone or something new — most noticeably a raft of new computers; a notice board where the cracked mirror had once been; a streamlined filing cupboard in the place of the old one with the drawer that stuck — and she felt suddenly disoriented and nostalgic for her past.

'You'll notice some changes,' Noakes, the duty sergeant told her.

'As long as no one's pinched my desk

I'm sure I'll pick up just where I left off,' Casey replied.

She'd worked out even before she went off on leave that it would be vital to respray her territory the minute she got back. She knew what the gossip about her would be, simply because she'd heard the same rubbish trotted out on those other occasions when fellow officers returned from maternity leave.

No doubt they'd been saying that her heart wouldn't be in it any more; that she'd be more unwilling to take risks now she had a child. Someone somewhere might even be running a book on how long it would be before she gave up policing altogether and became a full-time mum. Well, they'd better forget all that rubbish, because Casey Clunes was back to show them it was business as usual.

'I thought today you might want to familiarise yourself with the new computer software,' Noakes said.

Casey did a double take. 'Oh, come on, Noakesy. Have a heart,' she said. 'Can't you find me something a bit more interesting? What about the washed up body? Who's dealing with that?'

'Out of our hands at the moment, I'm afraid,' Noakes, said. 'Waiting on the M.E.'s report and you know how long that can take.'

'So we don't even know who he is or how he ended up in Keeper's Cove?'

''Fraid not.'

'Pity,' Casey said. 'But in that case I might just pop along to the morgue myself and have a sniff round.'

Sergeant Noakes wrinkled his nose, fastidiously. 'You haven't changed, have you, Casey?' he said. 'Still chomping at the bit?'

'I've had a baby, Noakesy. Not undergone gender reassignment surgery. Now, please, give me a proper job. None of this software update rubbish.'

Noakes, an experienced officer where bloody-minded C.I.D. were concerned had never for a second thought he'd succeed in tethering Casey to a computer — even for a fraction of her first day back in harness. But it had been worth a try, he thought, as, with a sigh of resignation he handed over the details of the case he'd known all along she'd end up with.

Ten minutes later, relishing the familiar feeling of being behind the wheel of a police car, Casey was on her way to the hospital to have a word with Mr Zane Bandali, who'd been kept in overnight. There were so many gaps in his statement, so Noakes had said, that questioning him had been a complete waste of time.

That was what a knock on the head did for you, Casey mused, driving past the Alamo Amusement Arcade — or what was left of it. On an impulse she pulled over. A couple of uniform were standing outside to deter anyone who might fancy having a poke around the rubble. She didn't recognise either of them — which meant she was going to have to waste valuable time introducing herself.

If she'd hoped to effect a pass with her Police I.D. her hopes were immediately dashed. No one was allowed inside, the shorter, stockier of the two P.Cs. said, in his South Wales accent.

'Forensics, see,' he said, apologetically. 'They've only just gone in themselves.

Hot as hell in there still, up to about a couple of hours ago.'

'So, they'll have no idea about the cause yet, then?'

'It'll be some gang thing, if you ask me,' the officer replied, pessimistically. 'Brockhaven's becoming a hotbed of crime and that's a fact.'

Casey did her best to hide a smile at his description of the sleepy seaside town they both policed.

'Come here from London, I did, for a bit of piece and quiet. Fed up with living life on the edge, know what I mean? But since I got here there's been all manner of dodgy dealings.'

Casey was on the point of choking. She couldn't imagine what crimes might have been committed in her absence to transform Brockhaven into the lawless wasteland of P.C. Jones' experience.

She made a mental note to look through the files as soon as she got back to the station to check if there'd been an increase in bicycle theft or parking offences while she'd been away.

'Who owns this place?' she asked.

The two officers exchanged questioning glances and shrugged. The Welsh officer had the idea it was a local man, while the other, local himself from his accent, disagreed. Definitely an outsider, he said, adamantly. Which, could have meant he came from five miles away or the other side of the world, since there'd have been little difference to a true native-born Brockhavener.

Casey decided to leave Mr Bandali for another hour or so. She justified it this way — if he'd been groggy last night, then the more time he was given to come round and apply his weakened faculties to the previous evening's events, the more clearly he'd remember it.

She was far more exercised about the washed up body. Of course, the chances were it was more likely to be either an accident or suicide than murder. But if there was anything even remotely suspicious about this case then she intended being the first to ferret it out.

On her way out of the station earlier she'd glimpsed Tony Lennon coming in through another door. Not exactly her rival — Casey was senior to him, which was something that had always rankled him — but he was ambitious and if there was any way he could cut her out of a juicy investigation and get the glory for himself, then Casey knew he wouldn't hesitate. So would she with him, of course. All was fair in love and war, after all.

Tony Lennon had hardly been an oil painting but she'd never thought him actually unattractive until she'd seen him this morning. Now he had jowls; he'd put on weight everywhere else too and his unshaven face and crumpled clothes gave him a dishevelled look that bordered on the sinister. Maybe he was ill? For all there was no love lost between them she wouldn't have wished that on him.

As she swung her car into the car park of Brockhaven and District Morgue, which, from the outside gave no hint of its internal macabre workings, being light and airy and welcoming, she made a mental note to get to the bottom of Lennon's metamorphosis. W.P.C. Gail Carter, font of all office gossip, would be the one to fill her in as far as Lennon was concerned.

Casey's heart sank when the girl on reception informed her that Dr Draper was the M.E. on duty today. She'd had dealings with him before. He was a dour, unyielding man, a doctor of the old school who would have expected God to doff his cap at him.

He had little time for the Police and even less for female officers. Casey had long since classified him as a dinosaur, whose only saving grace was that he'd be retiring soon.

If it was possible to judge a man's mood from the sound of his approaching footsteps then Dr Draper was irritable, bordering on the furious. An accurate conclusion that was quickly proved by his scowling face.

'I wondered how long it would be before you lot were round here hammering on my door,' he snarled.

Casey stood her ground. She'd confronted murderers and rapists in her time. She wasn't going to be put off by the likes of Dr Draper, who thought a Public School education and letters after his name were a substitute for good manners.

'Just on the off chance, Doctor. The sooner we know who we're dealing with the sooner we can inform next of kin.'

Casey could only conclude that her polite manner and gentle smile must have released an echo somewhere in the depths of Draper's psyche that here was a member of the fairer sex and that he perhaps ought not to be baring his teeth at her.

He changed stance from pugilistic to affable joker. Casey wasn't fooled. There'd be a sting in his words, if her past experience of the man standing before her was anything to go on. That sneer was never very far from his face, no matter how he tried to disguise it.

'I blame C.S.I. Miami or whatever it's called,' he drawled. 'You people seem to think a post mortem can be undergone while the medical officer in charge is eating a sandwich and the results known before he's finished it.'

You lot. You people. Did he talk to his wife and kids like that, Casey wondered.

'As if food would ever be allowed or

one would feel like eating it, given the surrounding circumstances,' he added, absent-mindedly.

'Haven't time for TV myself,' Casey replied, mock-affably. 'Much prefer a good concert on Radio 3. Or a nice biography.'

This was a complete fib — since Finlay's arrival even Coronation Street and the celebrity mags were over-taxing. But it was too much of a temptation not to try to bring Draper down a peg or two. She handed him her card.

'Soon as you know anything,' she said. 'Ring me, will you?'

Grudgingly he took it, read the contents — an achievement in itself, Casey thought — then slipped it into the top left hand pocket of his crisp white coat.

'I promise you'll be the first to hear,' he said, with what could only have been described as a coy smile.

Heavens to Betsy, Casey thought, as she nosed her car back into the late-morning traffic. Unless she'd misread the signs, she'd gone and got herself an admirer — albeit through her false assertion that she was a culture vulture. Just wait till she told Dom.

* * *

It was almost lunchtime and so far today Casey had achieved zilch. During a brief bout of self-doubt as to the wisdom of going back to work with Finlay so tiny, she'd comforted herself with the thought that her job was the one area of her life where she'd be allowed to finish one thing then move on to the next — so much less frustrating than looking after a baby, where tasks overlapped only to be repeated in a never-ending daily round.

But now the same merry-go-round was being repeated here at work. She'd got nothing from her visit to the amusement arcade and even less from her conversation with Draper — unless you counted the possibility that the odious doctor might possibly have taken a shine to her.

And now, after a futile trip to the hospital, where she'd been informed that Mr Bandali had discharged himself after breakfast, here she was standing in his tiny cluttered living room, getting nowhere again.

Casey was angry on the assaulted man's behalf. But she couldn't help but be angry with him too. What was the point, he said, of issuing a description? Nothing would be done to catch the men. Nothing ever was. Casey had to bite her tongue in order not to snap back that if he was unwilling to co-operate with the Police then what did he expect?

His tiny sari-clad wife, wedged between boxes of cigarette cartons on the settee, must have read her expression.

'We gave the CCTV to the other officer who was here,' she said.

Well, that was something at least. Though CCTV was vastly over-rated in Casey's opinion. There were blind spots; faces and forms came over as blurred images and wrongdoers, aware of the probability of the camera came dressed prepared. More importantly, CCTV couldn't pick up accent or what was said.

'It would be really helpful if you could give me a proper statement though, Mr Bandali,' Casey coaxed, in the same tone she used when she was trying to get Finlay to try a bit of food he'd never sampled before.

'I already told someone, last night,' he said.

Casey retrieved her notebook and took from between its covers a copy of that statement. It ran to four lines.

'At 9.30 on Saturday April 18th I was refilling the shelves. I was the only person in the shop. My wife was upstairs. I registered someone coming in so I got up, but it took me a moment because I'd been on my knees working on the lower shelves. Next thing I felt a blow to my head and I fell down again. That's all I remember.'

Mr Bandali listened attentively as Casey read the statement out. When she finished he shrugged his shoulders. 'That's it,' he said, his voice sullen.

Casey gathered all her reserves of patience. 'Sometimes, Mr Bandali,' she said, 'after a period of time has elapsed, other memories start to come to the fore.'

'Well not in this case,' he said, his whole demeanour suddenly challenging.

'I've told you all I know and now, if you don't mind, Inspector, I have a business to run. As you can see, we've just had a delivery and we need to get it on the shelves.'

Casey's eyes swept the room at the columns of stacked cardboard boxes. She couldn't help feeling relieved to learn that the Bandalis weren't sharing their living quarters with all these tins and dry goods on a permanent basis.

'Perhaps my wife can show you out,' he said.

Mrs Bandali struggled to her feet, dislodging a couple of boxes that collapsed into the space she left behind. Casey followed the tiny lady out and down the stairs to the front door of the shop. She was puzzled as to why Mrs Bandali appeared so calm. Her shop had been robbed and her husband assaulted, for God's sake.

'Please be assured, Mrs Bandali, that we'll do all we can to catch these villains,' Casey said, on the doorstep.

'Oh, don't worry, miss,' Mrs Bandali said. 'I don't think they'll come again.'

Casey's nose gave a metaphorical twitch.

There was much more to this robbery than met the eye, of this she was convinced.

'How do you mean, Mrs Bandali?'

Mrs Bandali tugged at her headscarf and covered her mouth with it. 'Because they know you'll be watching, of course,' she said.

I expect I'm going to have to make do with that explanation, Casey mused, as she turned on the engine and headed back to the station for some well-deserved lunch.

* * *

'Gail!' Balancing her tray, Casey headed over to W.P.C. Carter's table.

'My goodness,' she said, setting it down. 'You look more frazzled than me. And I've just had a baby.'

Gail grinned at her, gesturing for Casey to take a seat. 'So how's your first day? D'you think you'll be back tomorrow?'

'Things haven't changed,' Casey said. She lifted a wilted lettuce leaf from her plate and poked about underneath it. 'Still getting away with murder in the canteen, I see.'

'Got any baby photos?' Gail wanted to know. 'I haven't seen him since he was two months old.'

Casey dismissed the request. Later, she said. She was dying to know what had got Gail so frazzled.

Gail groaned. 'I don't know whether to blame Sandra Peters or Tony Lennon,' she said. 'They're both as bad as each other. Except he's a serving police officer and should know better.'

'I saw Tony earlier,' Casey said. 'He looked dog rough, and that's generous.'

Gail glanced round to check for anyone listening.

'Marital problems,' she mouthed. 'June's left him.'

Casey had only ever met June Lennon occasionally, at Christmas dinners and the like. But she'd liked what she saw. She was her own woman, with a neat line in put-downs who refused to be impressed by tales of derring-do Tony and some of the other lads would often launch into once the effect of the free booze kicked in.

'No way! What happened?' she said.

Gail shrugged. 'Lennon and me were

never particularly close,' she said. 'To be honest, the way he's acting these days he's doing a fine job of alienating the friends he *has* got. Since June left he's become a real loner.'

'So, tell me about him and Sandra Peters just now.'

Gail began her tale as Casey launched herself into her salad.

'Came in looking for her husband. Aidan. You know what she's like. Shouting the odds.'

Casey nodded. Sandra Peters was big, brash and loud. But she was a loyal wife. Casey should know, the number of alibis she'd given her husband over the years.

Aidan Peters was a well-known small time crook, noted for his incompetence. The number of times Casey had collared him was legion. Breaking and entering, fencing, affray. Poor Aidan Peters was rubbish at all of them.

'Said he hadn't been home for two nights.'

'He's not banged up then?' Casey was surprised. 'Must be a record. I tried to nick him for shoplifting just before I went off on leave but miraculously he got away with it.'

Gail grinned. 'They seek him here, they seek him there,' she joked. 'Anyway, she was kicking off. Said she'd rung up twice already to report him missing and got nowhere and that if he'd not had a record we'd be taking her more seriously.'

'So where does Lennon come in?'

'Round about the time the Sarge and I had finally calmed her down and promised to look for him. She was on her way out in fact, when he turned up. *Still looking for that waste of space, are you, Sandra?* he said. *What is it, gone off with the housekeeping, has he?*'

Casey rolled her eyes. When she heard her phone ringing from deep inside her bag, her stomach flipped. Not Debbie, she prayed. She groped for it as Gail continued talking.

'That was when she went for him. Both Noakesy and I had to pull her off him. Didn't blame her — though of course I had to read her the riot act. Lennon just brushed himself down and strolled off with a stupid smirk on his face. He'll overstep the mark once too often if you ask me.'

Casey had finally located her phone — a number she didn't recognise, which meant that Finlay was still safe at home with Debbie, thank God, and not in hospital on life support.

'It gets better you know, once you've got used to being away from them.'

Was it so obvious she'd been worrying about Finlay? Then she remembered Gail was a mum herself.

'It's me, Inspector. I am the bearer of news.' It was Dr Draper. 'Something interesting has come to light.'

'I'm listening, Doctor Draper.'

'Luckily, our victim's prints are on record so identifying him has been easy.' Draper paused for effect. 'His name is Aidan Peters,' he said.

Casey thought of Sandra, out looking for him and her heart went out to her.

'Much more interesting is the fact that Mr Peter's lungs contained very little water.' His glee billowed out into Casey's ear. 'You do know what that means, don't you, Inspector? In layman's terms?'

Oh, yes. She knew all right. It meant that Aidan Peters had lost his life through some other means, before he'd hit the water.

* * *

Casey crept upstairs and into Finlay's room, all in darkness apart from a sprinkling of fluorescent stars peppering the ceiling. Dom had painted the walls cream, to avoid any gender issues, he'd explained. But as soon as he discovered he'd become the father of a boy, he'd reverted to stereotype and added a frieze of aeroplanes.

The mobile above Finlay's cot — a carousel with horses and carriages poised for their next circuit — was every colour of the rainbow, but the dolphin-shaped lamp on Finlay's chest of drawers was pure baby boy blue.

Casey loved to watch him as he slept, his breath soft and even, his lashes — that curled so dramatically — resting on his plump, rosy cheeks. He was growing up so quickly. Already his hand had lost that starfish shape tiny babies had. Now she could see his fingers would be long and slim, like Dom's, not short and stubby and practical, like her own.

It had come as a big surprise to Casey that she'd given birth to this bouncing nine-pound boy. She was an only child, with only female cousins and had assumed she'd have a daughter too. For about two seconds, as the midwife laid him in her arms, she'd been in shock. There was no way she'd ever be able to mother a *boy*. But then his eyes found her face and claimed her. And that was that. Now it was impossible to imagine life without him.

Finlay stirred and Casey resisted the urge to stroke his fluffy head. Now she was back at work she sometimes felt she hardly saw him and had thought about encouraging Debbie to let him sleep more during the day so he could stay up longer.

Dom had knocked that idea on the head pretty swiftly, however. Hadn't they sat horrified through enough episodes of Nanny 911 not to have learned that babies thrived on routine?

Casey smiled. If she couldn't get a

cuddle from her son, then she'd go downstairs and get one from Dom, alongside the very large glass of red wine he'd promised her once she'd looked in on Finlay and got out of her funeral black. She didn't know which would be more welcome. Today had been a hard one, and that was a fact.

When news had begun to filter through that Aidan Peters' body had been washed up at Keeper's Cove there had been shock, but no one at the station had shed any tears. The received opinion was that Peters was a scrote and that as a result of his demise the residents of Brockhaven would now sleep more safely in their beds.

Tony Lennon had been the most voluble on this point. In fact, she might not even have gone to Peters' funeral in the first place had it not been for Lennon's scathing reaction to her suggestion — lightly made at first — that it might be a good idea for one of them to attend in order to pay their respects to his widow.

After all, Sandra had done her bit

— reporting Peters missing — on at least two occasions. And they'd fallen into the trap of taking no notice, more than likely just because her husband was an ex-con, as she'd suggested herself.

But it wasn't just provocation from Lennon that had strengthened her resolve. She'd been unable to discount the fact that though he'd been a criminal — albeit a pretty rubbish one on the whole — Aidan Peters was a dad too, like Dom. And his death meant he'd left three fatherless children behind.

As she sipped her glass of wine, comfy at last in tracksuit bottoms and one of Dom's cast off hoodies, Casey recalled the last occasion she'd brought Peters in. She'd been just about to go off on maternity leave at the time.

She smiled to herself as she remembered how he'd justified joining his chosen profession in the first place.

'A man's got to put bread on the table,' he'd said. 'If it hadn't been for the kids and the missis I'd have gone in for something with less anti-social hours, let me tell you.'

Anti-social being his euphemism for *thieving*, of course.

'You'll soon see for yourself what an expensive business bringing up nippers is, Detective Inspector Clunes,' he'd sighed, casting a glance at her tummy.

Casey had always believed in getting the suspects in and getting to the bottom of things as quickly as possible. She had a case load that weighed more than the weekly weight loss at Bockhaven's Slimming Club and wasting time on chit-chat was not the way to get on top of it.

But pregnancy had softened Casey. She'd slowed down. Even got a bit sleepy — particularly after lunch. She may not have managed to get a conviction the last time she'd had Peters in the interview room, but she'd learned an awful lot about his family while she'd been sitting back and allowing him to rabbit on, uninterrupted.

At the time she remembered thinking that though she hadn't met them yet she had a feeling — destiny being what it was — that it was more than likely their paths would cross eventually. Though she hadn't imagined for a minute that it would have been at their father's funeral.

Once the details of Aidan Peters' post-mortem had been released, Casey's determination to attend his funeral hardened. It had been impossible to be one hundred percent sure what had killed him, the report stated, as his lacerations and bruises — internal and external — could equally have been caused by the buffeting he'd received in the strong waves or from infliction by a human hand or weapon.

But one thing was certain — his lungs had contained far too little water for drowning to have been the cause. This was murder all right and low-life or not, Aidan Peters deserved justice just as much as the next man. On that point Casey would not waver, whatever the received opinion in the canteen might be.

Typically, on the afternoon of the funeral, the first person she'd bumped into as she'd been signing out was Lennon.

'Where are you off to in your finery?'

He looked mightily hung over, Casey

decided. A film of perspiration had settled on his brow. Had he broken into a sweat just from the effort of walking here from his car, parked outside, Casey wondered? If so she worried for his fitness levels.

June might have dumped him, but he'd obviously found a substitute companion, Casey decided — the bottle. It occurred to her that she'd been back a fortnight and he'd not yet asked her about Finlay. Was that just men or was it Lennon in particular?

When she told him where she was going his face cracked into a ghoulish smile. 'Well I suppose it's understandable you'd want to make sure he was definitely dead,' he said.

'Still delivering the wisecracks, eh, Tony?'

'I try,' he said.

Oh, yes, he was very trying, all right.

'I hope you've locked your wallet in your desk drawer,' he called out to her retreating back. 'Or one of his kids'll have it off you before they've carried his coffin in.'

'Laters, Tony,' Casey said, raising her arm in a farewell salute.

Brockhaven Crematorium was an uninspiring place, Casey always thought. When her time came she wanted a church and organ music, and a grave with a headstone and as much pomp and circumstance as Dom could deliver — provided she went first, of course. She reasoned that since so far she hadn't had a wedding day her funeral might be the only time she'd get to play the starring role.

The service was equally unexceptional. A grey-haired vicar spoke some words about a man it was obvious he'd never met. If he had then he never would have described Peters as *innocent*, Casey thought. The only thing Peters was innocent of was caring two hoots about the rising cost of the insurance premiums foisted upon his victims once he'd paid them a visit.

Was his murderer — or murderers — present now, beneath the chapel roof, wondering how much longer they were expected to sit and endure the Vicar's panegyric? Surreptitiously, Casey glanced around at the congregation. You could count the well wishers on the fingers of both hands and that included herself.

There was Sandra, small and thin and round-shouldered, sitting sniffing in the front row, flanked by a younger, taller, prettier version of herself — Sky, the teenage daughter no doubt — and an anonymous dark-suited male, a relative probably. There was no sign of the two younger children.

The man, keeping his eyes forward, scrabbled in his pocket for a tissue. Sandra took it from him with a fumbling hand. A gentleman, Casey couldn't help thinking. Whose side of the family was he on, she wondered. Sandra's or Peters? Or was he just a good friend . . . ?

Someone was shaking her, calling her name. Didn't they know to keep their voice down inside a holy place?

'Casey, Casey. Wake up. It's time to go to bed.' Dom was smiling down at her, holding out his hand to help her up.

* * *

Next day was Casey's day off — which, since Finlay had come along, she'd rapidly discovered was a bit of a euphemism. They'd been swimming and were now en route home via the supermarket, since, as usual, they'd managed to run out of several essential items even though Dom had done a big shop only a few days previously.

Casey strapped Finlay into the car seat, then dumped the bags in the boot. Something was bugging her. Last night, relaxing with her glass of wine, she'd been on the verge of making some connection in her head — something to do with Sandra and the tissue. Then Dom had gone and spoiled it with that nonsense of his. Of course she hadn't been snoring. How could she have when she hadn't even been asleep?

The worst thing you could do when you were desperate to remember something was to give it your full concentration. Let it go and it would creep up behind you when you least expected it, tap you on the shoulder and say your name.

'Hi, Casey! It is you, isn't it? I thought I caught a glimpse of you over in the household cleaning products aisle. Oh, sorry, did I startle you!'

The speaker, clearly startled herself as Casey spun round to face her, took several steps backwards. It took a moment before could Casey work out who it was.

'June!'

Finlay, unhappy about being ignored for all of three seconds let out an impatient yell. June ducked her head inside the car.

'No! I don't believe it! Last time we met you barely had a bump.'

'He's nine months now,' Casey said. The spaces between Finlay's yells were getting fewer.

June reacted with the appropriate expression of wonderment. 'He's lovely,' she said.

'Tired though,' Casey said, casting him an anxious glance. 'The trick is to start moving before all the little silences between cries join up.'

'I remember,' June said. Funny, Casey hadn't even known that June and Tony Lennon even had kids.

Thinking of Tony reminded Casey that

there was an elephant hovering between them that wasn't going to budge. On the spur of the moment, she decided it was time to draw attention to the beast.

'Listen, June,' she said. 'I'm sorry to have to rush off without being able to chat properly, but before I go I just want to say how sorry I was to hear about you and Tony . . . '

Finlay was now at full pitch.

June cast her eyes to the ground, obviously unwilling to discuss it.

'It can't be easy, being married to someone in the Force,' Casey went on, all the while wishing she'd left it at *sorry*.

June's smile was tight and formal. Motioning her towards her car, she said, 'You'd better get off before he screams the roof off.'

Glad of the excuse to get out of the embarrassing hole she'd dug for herself, Casey turned on the engine. Immediately she was struck by how cowardly she must look dashing off like this. She leaned out of the window and called out, 'Give us a bell and we can go out for a drink, eh?'

'That'd be great,' June said, rapping the

roof of the car in a gesture of farewell. 'Oh, and next time you see my husband, don't forget to ask him how he's getting on with his new friends, will you?'

Puzzled, Casey put the remark in the box marked *later*. Finlay was all she could cope with right now. With a final wave, she indicated and pulled away. Miraculously, he stopped crying as soon as the speedometer crept up to thirty.

And one more small miracle occurred. Last night's elusive flash of insight returned and solidified. Tomorrow she'd make a visit to Sandra, the grieving widow. Find out a bit more about her relationship with the man who'd never left her side at the funeral.

It was the manner in which he'd handed her that tissue, before she'd even asked for it. You'd have to know someone pretty well before you performed such an intimate gesture. Worthy of a brother, perhaps? Or a brother-in-law?

But the thing was, Sandra Peters had neither. Casey had spent enough time half-listening to his tales of family life to be sure of that. So who was this man with his arm round Sandra's shoulder as her husband's coffin disappeared into the furnace? A lover perhaps? Someone who might want his rival out of the way who'd be prepared to get rid of him either alone or with a willing accomplice — Sandra?

Sandra Peters lived out on the Lowestoft Road on a small modern estate, which was already run down. She greeted Casey with a suspicious expression that Casey had long ago learned not to take personally. A small girl clutched her hand and gazed up at her with china blue eyes, a matching coloured dummy stuck in her mouth.

'You'd better come in,' Sandra said, when Casey had introduced herself. 'If you can get in, that is.'

Both floor and furniture were covered with toys, some of them looking brand new. How come the less money you had, the more of it you spent on your kids instead of on basics like food, she thought, not for the first time?

'This is Chastity, isn't it?' Casey chucked the little girl under the chin. Immediately she opened her mouth in a big, dribbly grin and her dummy fell out.

'You got her on a list already, have you?'

Sandra, arms akimbo, was in battling mood.

'Lovely cards and flowers, Sandra,' she said, refusing to rise to the bait. 'I wanted to offer my condolences at the funeral, only I didn't want to intrude. I hope you'll accept them now.'

Grudgingly, Sandra gestured to the one chair that was clutter free. Casey sat down.

'Well, I suppose that's decent of you,' she said. 'Considering what a lot of trouble Aidan put you lot through in life.'

Casey agreed that they'd been on opposite sides most of the time. But Aidan hadn't deserved to be murdered, for all that.

'How was your husband's mood, in the days preceding his death?'

'Happy. Like he'd shed years,' she replied. 'Kept telling me good times were just around the corner. Even promised me a holiday.'

'Weren't you suspicious?'

'Ask no questions and you get no lies, Inspector. That's my motto. Last time I had a holiday was when I was expecting Chastity and I had two weeks in Brockhaven General with high blood pressure'

Casey was getting nowhere fast. The time had come, she decided, to bring out the big guns.

'Can't have been too great for you, though, Sandra, being married to Aidan. Never knowing when there'd be another knock at the door and a Police Officer standing there telling you your husband had been arrested again.'

She threw a glance in Chastity's direction, who, having retrieved her dummy and stuck it back where it belonged, was busy dressing and undressing a dolly.

'Every mother needs a bit of support with three kids, don't they? Especially with the age gap of yours.' There was a boy, too, Casey remembered, round about 11. Brooklyn, that was it, after one of the Beckham's boys. Football mad, apparently. 'What do you do for company when their dad's inside?'

Sandra threw back her head and gave a cackle that rattled the rafters.

'You're not suggesting I've got a lover, I hope?' she said. 'Chance'd be a fine thing.'

'That man, the one at your side at the funeral. Who is he, Sandra?'

Sandra was no slouch. She was there already, Casey realised.

'Oh, my God, you do think that, don't you? And that between us we did Aidan in so we could be together. Dear, oh dear, oh dear.' She laughed, mirthlessly.

If there was a joke in this somewhere, Casey was missing it.

'How well did you know my husband, Inspector?'

Casey said she thought she knew him very well. She knew all the names of his children, for instance. And that he was an only child. Like Sandra herself.

Sandra shook her head, resignedly. 'So he didn't tell you about Aubrey then? Still pretending, even after all these years.'

'I'm not exactly sure . . . '

'Aubrey's gay, Inspector. Aidan and him were brothers. Estranged. Had been for years, ever since their father kicked

Aubrey out for his — lifestyle. My word, Inspector. Aidan's father had a few different ones. All of them offensive.'

'I didn't know that.'

'Aidan was always so scared of his father he wouldn't have dared go over his head and keep in touch, then it got too late. It was easier to disown him.'

That was *that* little problem cleared up, then. Of course, she could be lying.

'If you can let me have an address for him.'

'Sure.' Sandra found her bag, rifled through it and retrieved a piece of paper on which was scribbled a Brighton address. 'Came over for the funeral and left the next day. He's a lovely man but the thought of him wanting his brother's wife is so wide of the mark it's a joke.'

Another blank, then. She might as well go home.

At the door she attempted one final question.

'Have you any idea who might have done it, Sandra? Any at all? Because, frankly, we're stumped.'

'I wish I did,' she said. 'He never hurt

nobody. Apart from those he robbed of course. I bet there's a few of his victims wouldn't have minded taking a swipe at him. That Bandali bloke, for one. Shaking his fist at me the other day when I went in his shop. Refused to serve me, he did. Didn't want none of my family on his premises if they were anything like my Aidan, he said. Cheek of it.'

Casey pricked up her ears.

'Bandali? Older gentleman? Got a shop just off North Parade?'

Sandra furrowed her brow. 'No. Here. On the estate. Young bloke, he is. A bit too cocky if you ask me. Took it over from Betty only a couple of months ago. She was lovely, she was. Always give you credit. Not like him.'

Sandra was clearly miles away. It was a good time to leave.

* * *

'Is this about my dad?'

Hussain Bandali glanced at Casey's ID, then switched the *open* sign to *closed*. He looked decidedly twitchy, Casey thought.

'Not as far as I know, Mr Bandali,' Casey said. 'This is about a murder.'

The young man frowned, puzzled. Casey pulled a photograph of Aidan Peters from her wallet. She studied Bandali's face as his eyes slid over it, contemptuously.

'I know him all right. Shoplifter. I sent him packing twice. I said if it happened I'd call the police,' he said.

'Very generous of you, Mr Bandali,' Casey said. 'But why wait so long. Most people would have reported him immediately.'

'I don't want any trouble with the law, that's all,' he said. 'The man was harmless. Just a nuisance.'

'So you didn't threaten Mr Peters, at all, did you? With your own brand of justice, I mean?'

Bandali dropped one of the magazines with a thud and blinked owlishly at her.

'Whoa! Stop there, Inspector. I'm a lover not a fighter. I asked the man to go, that's all. Second time I told him to keep away and his family too. That's all. You ask his wife.'

'I already have, actually,' Casey said, with a smile. 'That's why I'm here.'

'And does she corroborate what I say?'

She nodded.

'So we can leave it at that, then?'

He turned his attention to his display of magazines and threw himself into the task of reorganising them. Casey decided to show herself out. At the door she stopped.

'Since you mentioned your father Mr Bandali, how is he, by the way?'

His reaction to what was an entirely innocent question took her by surprise. He seemed panicked by it, she thought, and completely thrown off balance.

'My father? Why? What's he been saying? Has he been in touch with you again?'

She reassured him that he hadn't. She'd intended popping back but with pressure of work and everything, she hadn't got round to it.

'Perhaps I'll pop in now, on my way back to the station,' she said, innocently.

'There's no need for that, Inspector,' Bandali said, his composure regained. 'I spoke to him earlier and I can assure you he is fighting fit.'

'Well, that's good to know,' she said. 'I'll leave you to your magazines, then.'

Once in the car, Casey sat there, mulling things over. Something wasn't right. At the mention of murder Bandali's reaction was what you'd expect of an innocent man. Curious, puzzled.

But as soon as Casey brought up his father he'd gone on the defensive. When she said she might pop round to see him again he'd been thrown into a panic. The disparity between the two different reactions was completely out of all proportion.

It just didn't make sense. Hussain Bandali knew nothing about Aidan Peters' murder, Casey was convinced. But he was hiding something. And she was going to find out what that was.

'Snacks, lies and videotape'

Casey drummed her fingers on the desk. The detritus of coffee cups and snack wrappings was reaching saturation point, but neither caffeine nor calories was doing anything to speed up her brain activity.

Surreptitiously she glanced over at Tony Lennon, sitting at his desk. His back was towards her so she could only see the back of his head. His too-long hair brushed the collar of his shiny suit jacket and though her eyes weren't that sharp, her imagination visualised the garnish of dandruff settling on his shoulders as he moved his head from side to side. Tasty.

He was on the phone to someone but she couldn't hear what he was saying. There was too much else going on — other conversations, brief explosions of throat clearing and coughs, telephones bursting into shrill life. And beneath it all, the pulse that kept the whole place alive, beat the soothing drone of the computers.

Lennon looked busy. But looking busy and achieving anything of any consequence were two completely different things, as she should know. She'd been sitting here since first thing this morning, trying to get an overview of all the incidents that had occurred in or nearby local business premises while she'd been off on maternity leave, and desperately searching for any connection between them all.

Under any other circumstances this would have been a doddle. But when you were treading on the toes of the experienced officer who'd been put in charge of coordinating said incidents — in this case Tony Lennon — then covering your tracks was paramount. What she was doing was bang out of order and she risked discovery at any moment.

She'd lost count of the number of times she'd clicked away from the page she'd been studying on her computer, or sneakily slipped the statement she'd been reading back into its buff coloured folder each time a colleague strolled by and stopped to chat, a covetous eye on her biscuit stash. Honestly, it was like working with kids, sometimes.

She stared down at her scribbled notes. It was as clear as day followed night that since Casey had gone off on leave — round about the time he'd split up with June — Tony Lennon had been coasting.

According to her list there'd been a dozen or so crimes committed on small retail outlets over the last six months or so. Here were details of an ice cream van turned over, for instance — the first incident in the chain of assaults, break-ins and robberies, culminating in the worst one, the torching of the amusement arcade.

Skim reading the statements she'd found them sketchy in the least and she hadn't even been able to lay her hands on the one the arcade manager surely must have given. She tapped her teeth with her pen — an irritating habit Dom was always telling her off about, though what gave him the moral high road in habits she had no idea. She doubted the man had ever picked up a towel from a bathroom floor in his life.

The bottom line was that none of these crimes had been solved. They'd just been shelved. The general consensus among victims seemed to be that it was 'just kids' and that 'no harm was done'. Or they hadn't seen anything so it was no use them trying to identify the perpetrators.

The same reaction she'd got from Bandali Senior. She'd been met with a similar shiftiness later, when she'd gone to see his son to follow up Sandra's allegation that he'd threatened her husband just days before his death — false as that turned out — and she'd asked after his father.

Why, Bandali Junior had wanted to know. *What's he been saying? Has he been in touch with you again?* A puzzling reaction, surely? What had he been saying about *what?* And why would he want to get in touch with the police again? To change his statement?

Whatever the answer, he *hadn't* been in touch with them again and only Mr

Bandali Senior himself knew why not. Everyone, she was convinced, was hiding something. Every single victim, if you went by these accounts, was holding something back.

Not just the dodgy ones either — the one-man bands like the ice cream van man and the hot-dog seller — who probably did nothing by the book. But the kosher ones too were acting like the three wise monkeys. Why did none of these people want to see justice done?

Casey's mind jumped to her visit to the Bandalis' cluttered flat above the shop. Mrs Bandali had said that she, personally, had handed over the CCCTV video of the assault to the 'other officer' on the night of the attack. But if that was the case, then where was it? If she could get hold of that then maybe she could solve one crime at least.

Casey glanced over at Lennon again. This whole business was a mess but if she confronted him and told him that she thought he hadn't been pulling his weight on this one then things would only get worse. She had to work with the man after all. And another thing — she got no pleasure from kicking a man when he was down — not even Tony Lennon.

There was only one thing for it. Besides going over all these past statements, she was going to have to do a bit of legwork. It wasn't going to be easy. Not just because she risked being discovered treading on Lennon's toes but because she was working flat out to get to the bottom of Aidan Peter's murder too.

She had a list as long as her arm of Peters' old associates and victims to interview and there were only so many hours in a working day. What was the name of that Welsh P.C., she wondered? Jones, that was it. He looked keen. The type of officer who loved the house-to-house nitty-gritty of police work. She'd have a word with him, see if she couldn't persuade him to do a bit of donkeywork for her.

He could make a start on Peters' old associates while she introduced herself to Kevin Horrocks who managed the arcade — after she'd paid another visit to Zane Bandali. Twice he'd been interviewed

— once at the hospital and once at home — and both times to no avail. Third time lucky maybe.

* * *

But when Casey arrived at the Bandalis' later that afternoon, her luck was out. It was Mrs Bandali who was behind the counter, her husband, so she explained, having left just minutes earlier for the bank.

There would be no point the detective waiting, she added, as he'd told her he wouldn't be back till six-ish. She was composed — almost smug — Casey thought, with none of her husband's evasiveness or her son's jitteriness. Obviously, she expected Casey to turn right round and leave. It was like a red rag to a bull.

'Well, no matter,' she said, smiling sweetly. 'You and I can have a little chat instead.'

'Like I already said, I was upstairs making dinner that night. I heard nothing. Saw nothing. I came downstairs because my husband hadn't come up for his meal.' Mrs Bandali's hand fluttered to her face. 'And there he was.'

'Where exactly, Mrs Bandali?'

'Why, where he told you, of course. On the floor, by the shelf he'd been stacking.'

Casey changed tack. 'Your son seems very anxious about his father, Mrs Bandali.'

Mrs Bandali narrowed her eyes, suspicious. 'What do you want with my son, Inspector? What's he been saying? He has nothing to do with this,' she said.

There it was again — that same remark. *What's he been saying?* She was convinced of it now, they were colluding. Like they were protecting someone. But who? Each other? A third party? And why?

The kindling of suspicion in her brain suddenly exploded into flame. Of course! Why hadn't she thought of it before? They wouldn't speak because if they did there'd be further repercussions. Just as there would be to the ice-cream seller, to the hot dog man and all those other small traders.

Some of them had needed just a reminder — a kick, a bit of graffiti — and once they'd learned their lesson, it was business as usual. Some of them avoided being a target altogether — Mr Bandali's son, for instance. Now that was interesting. How had he avoided his father's fate? By being amenable and coughing up first time? A lover, not a fighter. His words, not hers.

Unlike his son, however, Zane Bandali had put up a bit of a fight. And ended up in hospital for his pains. Not surprising he was reluctant to co-operate with the police in case it happened again. Or something worse next time.

This wasn't kids doing this. Unless she was mistaken this was a protection racket, operating right here on her patch, and very successfully too. Organised crime was getting a toehold in the community and its victims were fobbing off the Police because they feared what might happen if they squealed. And the Police had fallen for it!

She was appalled and ashamed that they'd let it get this far and frankly furious with Lennon for failing to see the connection himself. Too busy with his new friends, the bottle and the boozer, no doubt! Mrs Bandali was speaking again.

'If there's anything else you need to know I suggest you study the video I gave the other police officer,' Mrs Bandali said. 'Not that you'll see much,' she added, 'since they were all wearing balaclavas.'

Ah, yes! The elusive video. Now where the hell had that got to? Another cock up in a whole chain of cock ups. Records had shown her that first at the scene had been P.C. Jim Saunders. Casey had seen him about. Red-haired. A mass of freckles. Mrs Bandali described him perfectly when Casey asked her to describe the officer who'd turned up when she'd made her 999 call.

'So you gave the video to him, right?'

Mrs Bandali, who, if Casey wasn't much mistaken was starting to lose her cool, blurted out that actually she hadn't. She'd been in a state, she said, worried about her husband. It was only later, when she got back from the hospital alone, after he'd been admitted that she'd had another police visit — plain clothes this time — and had handed the video over to him.

'Can you describe this other officer, Mrs Bandali?'

Mrs Bandali shrugged. He wasn't the kind of man you'd look at twice, she said. Navy suit. Receding hairline. Face a bit — well, puffy and unhealthy looking.

Tony Lennon, without a doubt.

'So you gave him the video?'

'He demanded it. Wouldn't believe me, like the uniformed police officer did, when I told him there'd been no tape in the camera. He marched right up to it and ripped it out. Said I was perverting the cause of justice.'

Mrs Bandali was shaking now. Perhaps she was waiting for Casey to ask her why she'd failed to give the videotape to the P.C. Saunders in the first place. But Casey didn't need to ask. It was obvious.

All she'd wanted to do was protect her husband and her business and that's what she still wanted. Maybe she'd learned from her son that the best way to be left alone was to play ball.

But what the hell was Lennon up to, turning up on his own, demanding that tape then failing to log it? Had he just forgotten? Casey was wishing she could believe this simple explanation. But after what she'd just heard her instincts just wouldn't let her.

'Thank you, Mrs Bandali. You've been most helpful,' she said.

'Don't you want to stay and speak some more to my husband?'

'No, that won't be necessary,' Casey said. 'I've got everything I need for now.'

And then some, she mused, as she let herself out.

* * *

There were a couple of interesting messages on her phone. The first was from P.C. Jones, just to tell her he was working down her list of those known to Aidan Peters and had so far come up with nothing but he hadn't given up hope. Bless him, thought Casey.

The next was from W.P.C. Gail Carter. Sandra Peters had been in again asking for Casey in person and seemed agitated. Would Casey mind dropping by? She refused to speak to anyone else.

Next on her 'to do' list. But first she needed to talk to Kevin Horrocks. Urgently. This gang, whoever they were, started small time. Only if their 'customers' didn't want to play did they up the ante.

The manager of the arcade was no team player, obviously, or the amusement arcade would still be standing. He'd gone right to the wire and this was the result. A brave man, in her estimation. She looked forward to making his acquaintance.

* * *

Kevin Horrocks was a hard man to find. From the various builders, plasterers and electricians she'd tripped over inside the arcade, she'd gleaned he was likely to be in one or the other of the pubs that lined the street outside. She found him in the Sticky Wicket, staring morosely at an empty glass. He'd been there a while, the barman said, when she asked if he could point him out.

Oh, she was looking forward to this encounter. Finally, she knew she was getting there.

'Mr Horrocks?'

Slowly he lifted his head and met her eye.

'You and I have never met, but I do believe you've dealt with a colleague of mine.' Casey offered her hand, which he shook limply. 'Can I get you another one of those?' she offered. 'Because I think we've got an awful lot of catching up to do.'

* * *

Sandra was at the door even before Casey was properly out of the car. She strode up the path, wondering what the new widow had on her mind. Sandra looked agitated, so Casey quickened her step.

The kids were nowhere in the house but Sandra wasn't alone.

'This is Fozzer.'

Casey recognised the man. Charlie Foster, on a rare visit to the outside world from the Scrubs. He looked quite the dandy with his gleaming quiff and his cowboy boots. She moved his Stetson off the settee and sat down.

'No need to get up on my account,' she said. 'Nice to meet you again, Fozzer,'

'You too ma'am.'

Fozzer was Brockhaven born and bred but his accent belonged in Tennessee.

'I want you to look at what's on this phone. It's Aidan's. *Was* Aidan's I should say,' Sandra said, cutting through the pleasantries.

Casey was rubbish with technology. This was just about the flashiest phone she'd ever seen. It may well have belonged to Peters but she doubted he'd have come by it honestly.

'Show her, Fozzer.'

Again, Fozzer was up in a second, ready to do Sandra's bidding.

'Tell her how you got it,' Sandra said.

He was a man of few words, was Fozzer, but all of them were well chosen.

'Aidan Peters was my friend. He gave me this phone the night before he died. If anything happens to me, Fozzer, he said, I want you to take it and use the pictures I took as evidence. And I want you to promise only to show them to Inspector Casey Clunes.' He pressed a few buttons then handed the phone back to Casey. 'He was categorical about that. So here it is, Inspector.'

Casey was afraid to take it from him. But here, in Sandra Peters' front room, with both Sandra and Fozzer staring right at her, she had no choice. Her heart sank when she saw who it was in the picture message.

'You know him, don't you, Inspector?' Sandra said. 'That D.C. Lennon. The creep who insulted my husband.'

Casey nodded but she couldn't find the courage to meet Sandra's eyes.

'Tell her what else he said, Fozzer. About how he'd found out Lennon was bent. That he was taking bribes from that geezer from up North who was running a protection racket.'

'It's all right, Sandra,' Casey said. 'There's no need for Fozzer to tell me anything else. I think I get the picture.'

The irony of her words didn't hit her till she was on her way to the police station, the phone safe in her bag, having left Sandra and Fozzer behind to wait it out.

* * *

This was far too serious to deal with on her own. Casey knew she should leave it to the top brass. But there was Lennon, having a cigarette, just yards away from where she'd parked her car, back at the nick. Before they got to him she'd tell him just what she thought of him — and remind him that though he might think he was smart, she was smarter.

'All right, Casey? How's the nappy changing?'

She wasn't having that.

'How's Curtis, Tony?'

Lennon took a long drag of his cigarette. But he was looking worried — as well he might.

'Rob Curtis? You know? Friend of yours? The one you've been taking bungs from as payment for destroying the evidence of his nasty little crimes? The videotapes and the paper trail?'

Now she understood what June had meant when she'd asked Casey to enquire how her estranged husband was getting on with his new friends. She'd thought it was beer and spirits. But earlier this afternoon Kevin Horrocks had put her right.

Rob Curtis had come up from Manchester when things had started going wrong for him up there and settled on Brockhaven, where there was no competition.

One by one he'd managed to pick off the smaller businesses with little opposition. But then he'd got to Horrocks, and Horrocks just wouldn't play ball.

'I had a long chat with the manager of the amusement arcade this afternoon, Tony. Remember him? Made quite a few calls to you. When he got his windows put in once. And that time someone pulled all the sinks off the wall in the gents. There were other incidents too before the big one. The fire, I mean.'

Lennon took one last drag of his cigarette, before grinding it beneath his feet. His face was a mask.

'Why did you do it, Tony? You might as well tell me, because the Super's on his way down here now to arrest you. Was it just for the money?'

'I did it for June,' Tony said, morosely. 'To make up for the long hours I worked. So I could retire early and we could buy a nice villa somewhere in the sun, like she'd always wanted.'

Casey shook her head. 'No, Tony,' she said. 'Oldest trick in the book, that. Blame the wife. Was it June's fault that Aidan Peters had to die too?'

She scrabbled in her bag and pulled out the phone. This time she found the picture message easily. Fozzer was a good and patient teacher. Lennon made a lunge for it, but Casey was too quick for him.

'You want to leave off the fags and booze, Tony,' she said. 'They're making you slow.'

From the corner of her eye she saw the Super striding out. Gail was there too and Noakes, the desk sergeant. And wasn't that her new Welsh mate, Jones, in the rear?

'Bit of a nuisance that Peters. Always hanging about where you don't want him to be. We'll never know what he was up to at the Arcade that day — no good without a doubt. But he saw you, didn't he, Tony? Handing over a couple of videos and a stack of statements. Then getting something in return.'

Lennon grimaced.

'Took a couple of lovely snaps with this brand new camera, didn't he? Then came back to you later to let you have a glimpse.'

'Thought he could blackmail me. The low-life.'

'Takes one to know one,' Casey said. 'How much did you pay him by the way, before you decided you'd had enough.'

Lennon shrugged. There was no need to reply. She knew how much. Enough to pay for a second honeymoon for him and Sandra in Magaluf.

'Are you going to tell me how you killed him? You might as well.'

Lennon found his cigarettes and lit another.

'I rang him. Arranged to meet. Down

by the sea front on the cliffs. He wasn't bright enough to ask why it had to be at two in the morning.'

Lennon spoke sullenly. Reverting to police officer mode he added that they'd probably find evidence of both their DNA down behind one of the bathing huts that lined the sea front. He'd pushed him down there, from the cliff top. Peters had taken a bad fall and didn't put up much of a fight.

Casey read out the arrest formula with a heavy heart.

* * *

'Busy day?'

Debbie had left when Casey got home and Dom was sitting with Finlay watching TV. The two of them looked so wholesome sitting there after the filth she'd been rubbing up against today.

She dropped a kiss on Dom's head and opened her arms for Finlay, who gazed rapturously into her face.

'We arrested a murderer,' she said.

'Good.'

She shook her head. 'No, not good. He was a colleague.'

She told Dom about Lennon and as she talked and hugged her son the day ebbed away. Soon it would be supper, a bath for Finlay, bedtime and a story.

'You know,' she said, 'back when I was on maternity leave I worried that I wouldn't be able to cope with family life.'

'And now?' Dom said.

'Now I know I'll never be able to cope without it.'

Dom eased himself out of his chair. 'I'll put the kettle on, shall I?' he said, brushing her cheek with a tender kiss.

A Tough Workout

Casey eyed Dom across the room, from the battered old sofa in which she sprawled. Time was when they'd have curled up together instead of sitting apart, she mused. But parenthood had stirred up other emotions besides the usual ones of unbounded joy and bursting pride in Finlay, their joint achievement. A desire for one's own space for one thing, and a nasty competitive streak for another.

They were playing the game of *I'm more exhausted than you* and right now it appeared to Casey that Dom, draped over the other sofa, was winning. Although he had absolutely no right to, since *she* was the one who'd packed in a twelve-hour shift today whereas he'd been *working from home*. A euphemism for wasting time if ever she'd heard one.

She knew what it really meant. Chasing useless bits of information round the

Internet in the vague hope it would have some relevance to some article he was writing, interspersed with messing around on Facebook and waiting for the kettle to boil while staring out the window when he could have been emptying the dishwasher or writing a shopping list.

He'd adopted the pose of a consumptive poet, one hand flung over his brow, eyes shut fast and brow furrowed in contemplation — a brilliant tactic she wished she'd come up with herself. When he suddenly stirred, Casey — who'd convinced herself he was in the game for the long haul — was taken completely by surprise.

'Guess who I spoke to earlier?' he asked her.

She grunted, so as not give the impression she was actually awake and listening.

'Remember old Peter Timms? You met him at that cricket match just before Finlay was born?'

'I remember the cricket match. Lots of men in white flannels. Not sure I could single him out from the rest though,'

Casey said. 'I also remember we were there for hours and nothing actually happened.'

'It did, but only during your toilet trips,' Dom reminded her. 'Which, as I recall, were legion.'

'Ah, yes. Late pregnancy. Happy Days.'

Dom chuckled. 'Well, he's getting married. And he's invited us to the wedding. Owzat?'

'What, all of us?'

Dom nodded. 'Finlay too.'

'Who's the lucky woman?' Casey demanded. 'I hope she likes cricket.'

Typically, Dom couldn't recall the fiancée's name.

'Call yourself a journalist,' Casey teased.

She pulled herself up into a sitting position.

'It'll cost a fortune,' she said, glumly, itemising everything they'd have to shell out for between now and two months hence, the date the wedding was scheduled — a night in a hotel, as it would be taking place at the other end of the country, a present, of course, and three new wedding outfits.

Dom dismissed her concerns with a nonchalant wave of his hand. Finlay would need stuff, sure, but he could still get into the morning suit he'd worn at the last bash they'd gone to. Couldn't she recycle something old if she didn't want to go to the expense of a new outfit? Though he'd always been led to believe that women needed no excuse to go shopping.

She might go and have a poke about in her wardrobe, she said, uneasy at the prospect. Recently it had become a habit to leave her jeans unbuttoned after dinner. She'd tried to fool herself they'd shrunk in the wash but the brutal truth was that since she'd stopped breastfeeding she'd expanded. Unwinding her limbs she rose from her chair.

'Oh, you making a cuppa?' Dom said, the glint of victory in his eye.

Dammit! He'd won.

'Might as well, I suppose,' she conceded. Flippin' stupid game anyway. She hadn't really been playing to win this time or she'd have beaten him hollow. 'Biscuit with that, sweetheart?' she trilled as she left the room.

Just to show she wasn't one to bear a grudge.

* * *

Next day, Casey sat at her desk endeavouring to work out how she could adequately divide her allotted hours among her infernally large caseload. It might just work if she gave up all thoughts of going home at the end of her shift and cut out any paperwork. But other than that there was precious little else she could do.

She'd already given up proper lunch breaks, relying instead on waylaying any passing colleague en route to the canteen and asking them to grab something for her too. Preferably something that didn't require a knife and fork, since she needed her hands to turn pages, tap keys or speak on the phone.

Today she was munching an obscenely large baguette. The crumbs alone would have fed a flock of greedy starlings.

'Enjoying that?'

Why did people always ask you a

question just as you'd filled your mouth with food, Casey wondered. She eyed Gail Carter's Tupperware box cautiously. It overflowed with chopped, raw vegetables and there wasn't a carb within spitting distance.

'Hmmm, nyaaa, brrrr, crrrnch,' she replied. Which roughly translated meant she'd tasted better, but beggars couldn't be choosers.

W.P.C. Carter stood up from her desk and reached for a bottle of water from an overhead shelf. She was looking particularly trim in her policewoman's uniform today, Casey observed. Gail had a daughter just a few months older than Finlay — a connection that had bonded the two women, transforming them from mere colleagues into friends. It was nice to swap baby milestones and commiserate over broken nights.

'What have you been doing to make yourself so svelte?'

Casey had got through her baguette now. She marvelled at how simple a feat it had been and was ever so slightly ashamed of herself for the speed at which she'd polished it off.

'I've lost a stone and God knows how many inches from my waist and hips,' Gail said, proudly. 'I'm in size ten jeans now.'

Casey widened her eyes. Dammit, she was jealous. The last time she'd been in size ten jeans she'd been drooling over George Michael's picture on her bedroom wall. Which had turned out to be a bit of a wasted effort on her part, in retrospect, she mused, fondly.

'It's all down to putting in the hours at the Fitness Centre,' Gail said. 'I swim and go to the gym three times a week and take as many aerobics classes as I can fit in.'

Casey was impressed and said so. If only she had time to do just half of that, she said. But what with the Super breathing down her neck, demanding to know when she was going to get to the bottom of this current spate of house break-ins, plus the recent staffing cuts, which meant she was doing the jobs of two people, then the demands of family life on top of all that, there was no time left for anything else.

'Excuses, excuses,' Gail teased. 'If you want something enough you can always make time.'

Casey knew her friend was right, but it wasn't something she relished hearing.

'Look, there's a class later this evening. Why not come along? Annie — the teacher — is great! Young, hyper, really motivating.'

Gail's face, which had lit up like a Christmas tree at Casey's compliment on her new figure, suddenly dropped.

'Not that I'm suggesting you need to lose weight or anything, Casey,' she said. 'It's just, after what you said, anything that boosts energy levels is always a help.'

Casey reassured Gail she wasn't offended in the slightest. In fact she was well aware she needed to shed a few pounds. She told her about the wedding invite they'd just had. The previous evening, after she'd been beaten hollow by Dom in the *I'm more exhausted than you game*, she'd slunk off to the bedroom where she'd failed miserably to find anything in her wardrobe that was both dressy enough for a wedding and still fitted. It had been so depressing.

‘The only thing I felt comfortable in was a maternity dress I wore to a summer garden party when I was seven months pregnant,’ she said, pulling a face.

‘Well, there’s your motivation then,’ Gail said. ‘How about if we tootle along to tonight’s class together?’

‘Inspector Clunes!’

Striding towards her and sniffing the air for timewasters in that suspicious manner of his, was Sergeant Noakes, the Duty Sergeant. Casey had never been so pleased to see him as she was at that moment, although she was well aware that the printout he was clutching very probably contained details of yet another job.

‘To what do I owe the pleasure, Sarge?’ She fixed him with a bright smile.

‘I don’t think you’ll get much pleasure from what I’ve got here,’ he said, wafting it so vigorously it unbalanced the polystyrene mug that had held her coffee so that it rolled off the desk onto the floor. Fortunately she’d drunk the contents.

‘Another break in,’ he said glumly. ‘If

you're not doing anything I'd like you to pay a visit to the victim's place of residence.'

'I'm on my way, Sarge,' she said, her tone grim. 'Too bad about that class, Gail,' she added over her shoulder as she made her way out. 'It would have been a blast.'

Gail's disbelieving roar of laughter rang in her ears all the way to her car.

* * *

It said a great deal about Casey's preoccupation with the subject of excess poundage that the first thing she noticed in Thea Mitchell's neat, end of terrace house was the pair of trainers by the door and the second thing was that Ms Mitchell hadn't an ounce of spare flesh on her.

Snap out of it, Clunes, she told herself. She was here to investigate a break-in, not pick up slimming tips. Ms Mitchell led her through to her sitting room and offered her a seat, expressing surprise that they'd sent a D.I. round rather than a humble P.C. A forensics team had already visited her property and done something very scientific with something that looked like ant powder, she added, but she hadn't expected anything more than that.

Casey explained why. This was the fourth break-in in this area in as many weeks with the same M.O. and catching the perpetrators had become a priority. Thieves had forced open a door, or — as in this case — broken a window and climbed in before clearing off with any item they could fit easily into a bag and that looked like it might be worth something. And all in a very short space of time. Most of the victims, like Ms Mitchell, hadn't been out of the house for more than two hours at the most.

'One hour and forty minutes in my case,' Ms Mitchell said. She shuddered. 'Do you think they were watching the house? Waiting for me to go out so they could rob me?'

'Most break-ins are opportunistic, you know,' Casey said, in a bid to reassure her. 'You could have returned at any time while they were in the act, so they wouldn't have wanted to hang around longer than necessary.'

Her words seemed to perk Ms Mitchell up a bit.

'You've got a list of everything they took, so I've been informed,' she said.

Thea Mitchell jumped up. 'Better than that,' she said, moving quickly over to a small desk from where she snatched up a handful of photos and thrust them into Casey's hands. 'Look!'

A quick glance revealed them to be holiday snaps. Greece? Crete? You rarely got skies that colour in Brockhaven. Or trees that shape.

'Round my neck? Do you see it? It's a very unusual necklace, I'm sure you'll agree.'

Casey nodded. 'Beautiful,' she said.

An amber pendant on a gold chain. Not Casey's sort of thing at all — the nearest she ever got to a piece of jewellery was her watch — but Thea Mitchell, with her auburn curls and golden skin had carried this piece off brilliantly, if the photo were anything to go by.

'Do you think I'll ever see it again?'

'We'll check out the local jewellers,' Casey said. 'Of course, these days, with the Internet . . .'

'It could be anywhere by now,' Ms Mitchell said, wistfully.

A realist, Casey decided, as she thanked Ms Mitchell for her time and said goodbye, doing her best to avoid looking at the trainers that seemed to accuse her from the hallway.

* * *

In the end she'd succumbed to pressure and on her way back to the station after speaking to Thea Mitchell she'd taken a detour past the Fitness Centre and popped inside.

Rashly, she'd booked the aerobics class with Annie Kovac that Gail had mentioned. Even more rashly she'd arranged an induction session with a rather gorgeous young man who wore shorts and a T-shirt emblazoned with the words *Fitness Instructor*.

There was a moment just before setting off to the class that she'd almost chickened out. Finlay was teething and Dom couldn't settle him. But when she tried insisting the baby needed his mum, Dom had practically pushed her out the door.

This was no time to rubbish her deeply held convictions on the necessity of the parity in parenting roles, he told her. Get out there and kick some butt! His pep talk had worked wonders and she'd come out of the class feeling a great deal livelier than when she'd gone in, just as Gail had promised her she would.

But this morning it was a different story. Casey ached with every bone in her body. And she had to go through the whole punishing routine again later, at her gym induction. She was in the throes of gently peeling off her jacket in a manner that would cause the least amount of pain to her poor arms and shoulders, when Noakes loomed in front of her.

'I wouldn't bother taking that off if I were you,' he said. 'I want you to take yourself down to Brockhaven General.'

'Why, Sarge, you don't need to worry

about me.' She gave a mock grimace. 'It's just a little stiffness. I'm sure it'll wear off soon.'

Irony was lost on Noakesy. But it never stopped her giving it a go. It was her sense of humour that got her through the day, she sighed, as, gingerly she hopped back into her car.

From tomorrow, when Dom had fixed the chain on her old bike, she'd be cycling in. She was suddenly grimly determined to get rid of her excess poundage before this damned wedding they'd promised to go to.

* * *

Sergeant Noakes had described Nico Demetriades as a hapless have-a-go hero. He lay propped up in bed, the lower part of his face partially obscured by a medical dressing. His muscular frame coupled with the hairiness of his thick arms and the bit of chest that was visible, lent him an air of machismo that suggested the blue-striped pyjamas he sported — of which only the top half was visible — were Mrs

D's idea and definitely not his.

'I've been selling kebabs in my van in the market square for fifteen years now and I won't let a bunch of thugs with an air gun stop me from making my living,' he said, a defiant gleam in his eyes — eyes overhung with brows of such abundance they could have mopped up an oil spill, Casey thought.

Casey knew those kebabs well. They called to her down the years, succulent and glistening with fat and hot sauce. How many Saturday nights, as a single girl out with friends, had she ended the night's revels in the queue outside the kebab van? Alas, both for herself and Mr Demetriades, kebabs were off the menu for now.

'So, tell me what happened exactly, sir. The more information we have the sooner we'll catch your attackers.'

It was just after one in the morning, he said. He'd been cleaning the grill, just before closing up, when three men turned up, wearing hoodies and with what he supposed were women's tights over their faces.

'One of them spoke, demanding I handed over my night's takings,' he continued. 'I moved towards the door with the grill scraper in my hand. Although I had no idea what I meant to do with it. My mind just went blank.'

'I expect it was the sight of that in your hand that panicked them into shooting before they fled,' Casey said.

'Next time it won't be a grill scraper,' Mr Demetriades said, grimly. 'Next time I'll have something I can defend myself with properly.'

Casey shifted uneasily in her chair. Oh dear. It was time to deliver her usual reminder about the Law not looking too kindly on people carrying weapons on the off chance they might be attacked.

'So what are you suggesting? That next time I invite them inside and show them where my till is? Maybe throw in a kebab on the house for good measure?' He gestured operatically with his thick, hairy arms, his Greek accent growing stronger the more agitated he got. Hardly surprising his attackers fled, thought Casey.

'No,' she said, suppressing a smile. She

liked this man. Almost as much as she liked his kebabs. 'I'm suggesting you leave it to the Police.'

'If I thought the Police could catch them, I would,' he said, unconvinced.

'We will, Mr Demetriades,' Casey promised. 'These are amateurs we're dealing with. The fact that they were so easily scared and left with nothing and the way they reacted when you came after them all suggest it. If they'd been serious I'm afraid the outcome would have been a great deal worse than it is.'

'My wife thinks I was an idiot going after them,' he said.

'That's because she loves you,' she replied, which brought a boyish smile to Mr Demetriades' lips. 'Now, you get well soon. And don't you worry. You'll be back in your kebab van before you can say souvlakia with extra sauce.'

Mr Demetriades' smile broadened into a grin and he gave a bellowing laugh. Men, thought Casey, as she made her way out of the Ward. They were all softies at heart. You just needed to know how to handle them.

* * *

Let's not talk shop was the mantra Casey and Gail had adopted when they started socialising together. But it was inevitable that sooner or later, on a night out, they would. As they trailed up the steps to the dance studio, where Annie's class was about to start, they quickly found themselves catching up on each other's busy day.

While Casey had been at the Hospital interviewing Mr Demitriades, Gail had been despatched to interview yet another victim of a house break-in. There was a P.C. already on the scenc but the victim was throwing a wobbly and Noakes, in his infinite wisdom had decided that Gail, as a female, was better qualified to deal with the hysteria of a fellow female.

'You know what he's like.' Gail raised her eyes heavenward. 'No amount of evidence to the contrary will shift his belief that W.P.C.s are more qualified to make soothing cups of tea and offer a listening ear than male officers.'

'He's one of a kind,' Casey agreed. 'Thank God!'

The upshot of Gail's visit — and the only reason she was telling Casey this now and not leaving it till tomorrow that the victim — Charlotte Grainger — was, co-incidentally, a regular at Annie's class and she sort of knew her.

'I just wanted to forewarn you,' she said, as they pushed open the door to join the rest of the chattering women already gathered inside. 'In case she's here tonight.'

'Thanks for the heads-up,' Casey said.

Annie was already at the front of the class, marching her feet up and down to the music, calling out the moves and waiting for the class to join in. Hair scraped off her pretty young face, she was dressed in figure hugging sweat pants with a complicated arrangement of layers on her top half, all of which, apart from the final skimpy T-shirt, would come off, as the workout got sweatier, Casey knew from the last session she'd attended,

'Blimey, Annie doesn't hang about, does she?' Casey slid into a space between

Gail and a Rubenesque woman in her forties and began to march on the spot. 'Is she here?'

Gail was scanning the room for Charlotte Grainger as she too began marching.

'Not that I can see. Probably too upset. Worried they might come back, that sort of thing,' she said. 'Kept saying they must have known she was going out because she was gone for no time yesterday morning when they broke in.'

Gail stopped speaking at this point, needing her breath to keep up and her brain to engage with the complicated routines Annie always dreamt up. Tonight she was putting them through their paces at a lick so Casey too soon gave up looking for a woman of Charlotte Grainger's description and gave Annie her full concentration.

But then, someone she *did* recognise caught her eye a couple of rows in front. Thea Mitchell — trim in designer sweat pants and fancy trainers. Good for her for showing up, when anybody would have sympathised if she'd preferred to stay home feeling sorry for herself, Casey thought as Annie shouted her instructions.

Twenty minutes in now and the whole room was pumped. Casey had never been a natural mover and if her concentration lapsed for just one second, she often ended up going right when everyone else was going left and doing cheerleader arms when the rest were doing skipping rope ones.

But Annie's enthusiastic whoops of encouragement spurred everyone on. *What did it matter if you went wrong?* she'd yell periodically. *If you're moving your arms and feet it's all good*.

Finally the moment arrived when Annie had raised enough of a sweat to peel off her outer layer. She unzipped her long sleeved top, quickly pulled it off and threw it into the corner where it joined her bottle of water. A sudden flash and sparkle of bright gold and the glint of deep orange caught Casey's eye, stirring up something in her memory and briefly throwing her off her rhythm.

'Now we're going for it, ladies,' Annie cried, above the music, raising her arms high and punching the air. 'Whoo-ooo! Come on!'

But another cry came even louder, almost drowning Annie out. It was the sight of Thea Mitchell's contorted expression that came not from intense physical agony but from fury, that stopped Casey and everyone else, in their tracks. Only the music played on, indifferently.

Oh. My. God. Now Casey understood what had disturbed her. Thea Mitchell had seen it too. Her beautiful, elegant amber pendant. Rhythmically swinging from side to side around Annie Kovak's neck.

* * *

For a few seconds after Thea Mitchell brought the aerobics session to such a dramatic conclusion, the music carried on thumping out its driving beat. One or two women — each lost in her own little world — even continued moving their feet and arms, until it became apparent they were the only ones and so gradually they came to a sheepish halt.

Casey and Gail had immediately leaped

into Police Officer mode, with Gail leading a distraught Thea Mitchell away, to find her a cup of tea somewhere, and Casey deftly turning off the music without removing her firm grip on Annie.

Then, once she'd introduced herself to the class as Inspector Casey Clunes of Brockhaven CID, she announced that she was suspending the class for the evening and asked everyone to pick up their belongings and leave the room as quickly as possible. Now she was alone with Annie, who was obviously shaken by events.

'I really don't understand,' she said, when Casey assured her that the pendant was definitely Miss Mitchell's; she'd seen photos of her wearing it herself. 'How can it belong to her? I found it in one of my trainers, just yesterday.'

Casey gave a double take. Found it in on one of her trainers? It was a long time since Casey had believed in the Tooth Fairy.

'I know how it must sound.' Annie's fingers flew up to the pendant, as if to reassure herself that Thea Mitchell hadn't managed to make off with it. 'Let me explain.'

'You have my full attention, Miss Kovac,' Casey said. 'But before you do I am going to have to caution you.'

'You're going to arrest me?' Annie's eyes widened.

'Under the circumstances I have no choice,' Casey said. 'I think it would best too if we continued this little chat at the station. I don't suppose you have a solicitor, do you?'

* * *

Aaron Strummer wondered why one of his clients — Cass? Cassie Something? — the one he'd done the gym induction with recently, was leading Annie past Reception, where he lounged against the desk, exchanging the usual tedious banter with Terri, the Receptionist, who, annoyingly for him, never missed an opportunity to engage him in conversation.

The truth was, he thought Terri was a bit of drag. But he knew she liked him and looked forward to their chats and he could never have brought himself to just walk past without stopping and acknowledging her. It would have been cruel. All his friends said he was far too soft for his own good, so it must be true.

But now he had no qualms about cutting Terri off mid-flow. He sprinted after the two women, catching up with them just as they reached the exit.

'What's going on, Annie?'

Annie turned her face towards him. He'd never seen her look so miserable. He eyed the older woman nervously and gave her a nod of acknowledgement. Always be polite to the customers, he'd been told. The woman nodded back but didn't speak, like she was leaving it up to Annie whether she wanted to explain or not.

'It's nothing,' Annie said. 'Just a mistake. We're going to the Police Station to clear it up.'

'Police Station!'

He looked at the older woman again, this time with new eyes. And there he was thinking she was just another one of the bored housewives who made up his usual client list.

Although, perhaps he should have known she was different — there'd definitely been something about her. Couldn't put his finger on it, but when he'd shown her the equipment and encouraged her to have a go on each piece, there'd been none of that giggly silly-me behaviour he'd grown used to expecting from women of that age who were terrified of making a show of themselves.

Instead she'd just listened, observed, nodded her understanding or asked an intelligent question if she hadn't got it. He'd thought she was okay. But now here she was she was, for all he knew on the point of slapping Annie behind bars.

'You mustn't worry, Aaron. I've done nothing wrong. I'll be back in tomorrow.'

He wanted to do something — protest. He should have offered to go with her but by now it was too late — the two women had already been swallowed up by the night. So he just stood there, rooted to the spot, staring at the place where Annie had stood.

'Well, well, well!'

Terri was shuffling papers briskly. Her

wide-eyed, animated expression angered Aaron. It was as if she thought the whole episode was a diversion — a play put on especially for her amusement, to add a bit of sparkle to her day.

'What d'you mean *well, well, well*?' he snarled, forgetting his manners for once.

'Nothing,' she said. 'It was just a comment. I was just thinking about how it looked.'

Aaron felt hot with indignation. 'And how *does* it look?' he snapped.

'Well, there's no smoke without fire, is there?' she said.

Aaron had had enough. He wasn't going to stand here and listen to this slur on Annie's character. Brusquely he turned his back on the desk. 'I've got work to do,' he said, over his shoulder as he strode off in the direction of the gym. Wow, how good did *that* make him feel!

* * *

Casey had ignored the barely concealed expressions of amusement on the faces of the on-duty officers as she came through the Station door, dressed in her aerobics kit, with Annie in tow.

Hadn't they seen a pair of trainers and a tracksuit before, she barked? It might do some of *them* a bit of good to get down to the gym once in a while instead of spending their free time playing snooker and swilling pints.

'Now, I need someone to get onto the duty solicitor immediately and tell whoever's on to get round here ASAP, please.' She fixed a gimlet eye on the nearest P.C. who scurried off to do her bidding.

Finally, with legal representation in place, Casey allowed Annie Kovac to tell her side of the story.

'Let's start from where we left off back at the studio, shall we?' Casey said. 'You told me you found this pendant tucked inside one of your trainers.'

Annie Kovac still hadn't lost the look of bewilderment that had appeared on her face the moment Thea Mitchell had flung herself at her back at the studio.

'That's right. I teach lots of different activities so I need different shoes,' she explained. 'I should put stuff in a locker, but sometimes I just can't be bothered.'

'Didn't you wonder why it was there?' Casey asked her.

'Yes, I suppose I did.' She stared at the floor for what seemed an age. It was as if she thought there might be answer there, Casey thought. 'I thought probably someone had found it and slipped it into my shoe thinking it was mine.'

It sounded like a plausible explanation, Casey had to admit.

'I'm wondering why you didn't take it to Reception,' she said, 'instead of appropriating the item yourself.'

Annie averted her eyes. 'I probably should have done,' she muttered. Another pause. Then, 'I actually intended to,' she added.

'So why didn't you?'

'I suppose I just wanted to wear it once, that's all. It was so pretty.'

Her eyes alighted on the pendant, where — now bagged for evidence — it lay on the table between them. Then returning her gaze to Casey, she said, 'Please. You've got to believe me. I'm no thief.'

Casey longed to. It didn't make sense

to her. Why would Annie risk wearing such a distinct item of jewellery in front of her class, where there was a good chance that it might be spotted by the real owner?

It occurred to her that there could be a very good reason for Annie's discomfort and her reluctance to volunteer any information unless it was dragged out of her.

'You're not covering for someone are you, Miss Kovac?' Casey asked her.

'Of course not,' she replied, indignantly, her colour rising. 'It's exactly as I'm saying.'

'And you know nothing about a break-in at 10, Wilton Close on the fifteenth of this month?'

'A break-in? No, of course I don't. Is that where this pendant came from?'

Either she was a damned fine actress or she was telling the truth. Casey couldn't see Annie Kovac as a burglar — though she was limber enough to climb in through the smallest window — but that didn't rule out the possibility of a connection with the real culprits.

'There have been a number of items taken from various houses in Brockhaven over the last few weeks,' Casey said.

As she reeled off each address and the date of every break-in, Annie seemed to shrink further back into her seat.

'Do you know anything about any of these break-ins, Miss Novak?' Casey said, when she'd finished.

'No! Of course I don't! I'm telling you — I found that pendant in my trainers.' She was growing more and more distraught with every word she uttered. 'I have no idea how it got there but I certainly didn't break into anybody's house to steal it. And I didn't break into anybody else's house to steal anything else, either.'

The duty solicitor, looking decidedly anxious at this turn of events, cleared his throat. 'Inspector, are you going to charge my client?' he asked.

Casey glanced down at the pendant in its plastic bag, then at the Solicitor, before finally resting her gaze on Annie. She had no evidence to prove that Annie Kovac was connected to any of those other break-ins. But with the evidence of Thea Mitchell's amber pedant staring her in the face, could she allow this young woman to walk away scot-free?

If she was innocent and continued to maintain that she was, then it was up to a jury to decide. If she was covering for someone, then it was up to Casey to encourage her to reveal exactly who that person was.

'Under the circumstances,' she said, fixing the solicitor with a grim smile, 'I really have no alternative.'

* * *

There were days when Casey felt just useless and today was one of them. She'd been on a paper trail all morning and still hadn't caught up with it. She had a string of messages on her phone, none of which shed even the faintest beam of light on any of the cases she was working on. And, as usual, someone had phoned in sick, which meant they were a man down and she had even more to do than usual.

Only one message — the very last one

— was promising. She might have got somewhere with it if she'd been given the chance. But then, who should come bustling over but Noakes, making a fuss about last month's expenses claim. As if she had nothing better to do than keep receipts for every cup of tea she drank when she was on a job! Couldn't he just take her word that *about £1.30* meant just that? Flamin' jobsworth!

The message she'd got from Soco was that they'd found some evidence regarding the attack on Nico Demetriades. A glance at the clock told her that now it was far too late to ring back; they would all have gone home ages ago. Not everybody worked the same stupid hours as she did. Oh, well, she'd try again tomorrow, she decided.

Her thoughts returned to Annie Kovac. What did they know about her? She had no criminal record, she doggedly maintained her innocence and when her flat was searched the previous evening nothing incriminating had been found. Not even a Yoga mat or a pair of hand weights that were the property of the Fitness

Centre, apparently.

What did it all mean? The only way to get to the bottom of the whole affair was to play by the book and check Kovac's alibis closely. With a bit of luck they might come up with something that didn't quite tally with the story she'd stuck to throughout her interview and continued to stick with.

Sooner or later, if they kept picking at it they'd be bound to get under her skin. Maybe then she'd reveal just who it was she was covering up for. Because there was definitely someone else involved in this business, Casey was convinced of that.

'Penny for them!'

It was Gail, on her way in to start her shift.

'Urgh! Don't ask. My brain is mush. I'm going home to put my feet up and cuddle my baby.' It was the best idea she'd had all day, Casey decided.

'Have you been to the gym yet since your induction? I always find a session on the cross trainer sorts out my sluggishness. You could nip in on your way home.'

Casey pulled a face.

'I know, I know, I'm sorry,' Gail said. 'You must be getting fed up with me nagging you every time I get the chance. I sound like one of those born-again Christians.'

Casey grinned. 'Matter of fact the similarities hadn't escaped my notice, Reverend,' she quipped.

But actually it didn't seem such a bad idea of Gail's after all. What did she have to lose beside a few hundred calories? And exercise was good for the brain, too, right? It might be just the thing to trigger off a train of thought which — sooner rather than later — might lead to the unravelling of this mystery.

* * *

The interview with the Manager had gone badly for Annie. How could he have turned against her so easily? She'd worked here at The Fitness Centre for two full years and had never had a day off sick.

Customers loved her — she had the evidence of that in all those questionnaires clients were always being asked to fill in. But just because of that stupid pendant she was to be suspended.

If she'd told that Police Inspector everything she suspected herself about its mysterious appearance in her trainer she'd be in the clear and would still have her job now — the best job in the world. And not just because it allowed her to pass on her enthusiasm for keep fit to other people either.

One other factor made it so too. Aaron. And she'd sworn to herself that she would protect him until the opportunity came along for her to confront him with her suspicions. If they were correct, then they'd face what followed together. If she was wrong — well — right now she didn't think she had the strength to even go there.

Thank God she'd had the good sense to stash those other things in a locker and not take them home, was all she could think, otherwise she'd be up on several more charges.

The manager's final words rang in her ears, bringing her to tears this time.

I'm afraid that as long as you are under

suspicion I have no choice but to suspend you indefinitely.

It wasn't fair. It just wasn't fair. She flung open the door of the staffroom, praying for it to be empty. She didn't think she could bear any more humiliation right now. But it seemed even God was against her. There was Aaron, tall, bronzed and fit, relaxing with the newspaper and an energy drink. As usual when she saw him, her pulse began to race.

'Annie!'

Her eyes brimmed with tears. She must look so ugly, she thought. 'I have to empty my locker and leave the premises,' she said refusing to look at him in case she broke down completely. 'I've got fifteen minutes.'

Aaron jumped up, allowing his newspaper to flutter to the ground. 'But this is crazy!' he said. 'They can't do this!'

'Try telling that to the manager,' she said. 'Not to mention the Police. They've charged me WITH POSSESSION OF STOLEN GOODS. They've searched my flat. So it's obvious what they think.'

'And did they find anything?'

Aaron's searching gaze was the signal Annie needed and she seized it. She'd been waiting for this moment, ever since the first piece of jewellery appeared in her trainer, one gloomy Tuesday morning about a month ago.

Taking her courage in her hand she finally confronted him with the words she'd been practising throughout the previous sleepless night and for many nights previous to that.

'About those stolen objects. I think I should stop pretending I don't know how they came to be in my possession,' she said.

* * *

Gail had been right. After her workout Casey's mood was much better than it had been when she'd left the Station. She'd managed twenty minutes each on the cross-trainer and the treadmill, done a good deal of rowing and pulling weights and gone through all the floor exercises she could remember from her induction session with the hunky young man who'd taken her round.

It had crossed her mind, when he'd come rushing to Annie's aid the other day, that he fancied her rather badly. Not that he knew it yet. Men, in her experience, were a bit slow on the uptake. Mind you, now that Annie had been arrested and charged with theft he might soon lose interest in her. You couldn't blame him.

She was looking forward to the cycle ride home after her shower. Dom had spruced up the old bike brilliantly, fixing lights, panniers and a basket onto it. He'd even bought her a cycle helmet, but she'd told him in no uncertain terms that that wouldn't be necessary, thank you very much. *Vanity*, he replied, *thy name is Casey Clunes*.

The thing is, he was right. She *was* starting to get a bit vain since she'd begun this health and fitness kick, glancing in every mirror she passed and sucking in her tummy while thinking that, actually, she was already starting to look in better shape.

There was no way she was going to Dom's cricketing chum's nuptials in a maternity dress, the only thing in her wardrobe suitable for a wedding she'd felt comfortable in last time she'd tried it on. No, she was going to buy something new, in a smaller size and she was going to rock it fabulously.

And if that meant putting in more exercise and foregoing her lunchtime baguette, then so be it. She had no intentions of going down the elasticated waist route for several more years yet!

It was with all this in mind that Casey, quite on the spur of the moment, paused at the Reception desk instead of simply making her way out, having decided that perhaps she should make enquiries about pool opening times while she was here.

Unfortunately for her, it was exactly at this moment that Annie Kovac chose to come storming past Reception too, her face a mask of barely controlled grief and pain, as she headed towards the door.

Annie saw Inspector Clunes, whose back was towards her, before the Inspector saw her. Maybe if the Officer hadn't been there Annie would have allowed herself to simply creep away, go home and lick her wounds. But after the conversation she'd just had with Aaron she reckoned she'd been humiliated enough.

Before she lost her nerve completely she began to reveal the suspicions she'd been harbouring — that everything had come from him — the pendant, those opal earrings, the sweet bracelet, the watch with the funny face.

Did you put them there? In my shoes? she'd asked him. Still optimistic at this point; still hopeful he would own up. His look of bafflement disturbed her. It wasn't the response she'd anticipated when she'd rehearsed this conversation at home, alone.

Why on earth would I do that? he'd said. Not, *so you guessed?* which was what she'd hoped and dreamed of.

She should have left it there. Said, *oh, nothing*. Been nonchalant. But instead she'd ploughed on: *I've thought, all this time, that they were love tokens*. Making the situation worse.

Even before she finished her sentence she knew she'd got things badly wrong. She didn't wait to hear his reply. His face told her everything and in it she read all she'd dreaded knowing. Embarrassment, discomfort, awkwardness and pity — all were there.

But not the slightest trace that she'd been right in her assumptions. Hastily shoving the trinkets back into her bag, she turned and fled. Seeing that Police Officer loitering at Reception was the last straw,

'Have you come here to spy on me again?' she yelled. 'Why can't you just leave me alone?'

Casey spun round, caught off guard. The Receptionist, equally alarmed, drew in a sharp breath,

'Do you want me to call Security?' She leaned forwards, speaking in a confidential whisper, but Annie had heard her.

'No need,' she said. 'I'm going. And Terri, you can tell the Manager I've resigned. So there's no need for him to suspend me after all. I won't work anywhere where I'm not trusted.'

Then, with a last bitter glance in Casey's direction, she was gone.

'If that's not an admission of guilt, then I don't know what is.' The Receptionist spoke primly, the reflection of her computer screen causing the lenses of her glasses to glint.

Casey chose to ignore the remark. She wished she were so certain. What had upset Annie so? Was it just her presence or had something else happened to cause her such grief? Her instincts cried out that she should follow her outside — try to talk to her and get her to tell her everything she knew. But she'd been given the chance to do that at her interview and rejected it. Now she'd been charged with a crime. Chasing after her to speak to her off the record might jeopardise the court case.

Instead, she did nothing, simply waited for Annie to get right off the premises before she made her own way out, her thoughts turning over furiously all the while. So that although she was aware of the Receptionist's prattle, she barely caught a word of anything she said. She could only guess it was of Annie that she spoke in such a derisory manner.

Once she felt she could be sure Annie was no longer around, she left herself. It was while she was unlocking her bike that she was aware of someone coming towards her. It was her Fitness Instructor — she'd heard Annie address him as Aaron.

He looked awkward. Like he had a great deal on his mind but no idea where to start. She decided to give him a hand.

'Can I help?'

He hovered by the side of her bike, trying hard to get some kind of grip on himself.

'I have to speak to you,' he said. 'About Annie. I think there's something you should know.'

* * *

Dom swept Finlay up in his arms and planted a noisy kiss on his sweet button nose. In return — and just as affectionately meant — Finlay blew his father a symphony of raspberries, pedalling his plump legs furiously in accompaniment.

'Looks like it's just you and me again, buddy.' Dom blinked away the baby spit that had landed in his eye. 'Mummy's been delayed at the gym.'

Finlay grinned and gurgled. He was such an easy-going little chap, Dom thought, proudly, always just as happy to be left with Debbie, the nanny, or, as now, with himself. Good job, really, because with Casey for a mother, amenability was a characteristic that was always going to stand him in good stead.

As far as her working hours were concerned she was thoroughly unreliable and always had been. Trying to get her to give a set time when she'd be home was a bit like expecting to get an honest answer from a politician. But fortunately for little Finlay and for himself too, Casey was a hundred per cent reliable where it really counted.

Of course, that had its down side, too. It meant, for instance, that once he broached the subject he'd been mulling over ever since that damned wedding invitation had dropped into his inbox, he was ninety nine point nine per cent positive of the reaction to expect from her.

She'd fix him with that look — head on one side, slightly lopsided mouth turned up in a suspicious smile. Then, just as if he were one of her suspects, she'd turn over his words and examine them from every angle.

Both those things would be bad enough. But sooner or later she was bound to open her mouth and speak. *Are you out of your mind, Dominic Talbot? If it ain't broke, don't fix it*. He could hear the words already.

Dom sighed. Perhaps he should just forget the whole thing. But that was a coward's way out. Finlay burbled a little song and smiled his sunny smile and as usual it melted Dom's heart. He guessed that in Finlay's small world he, as his father, was right at the centre. What kind of an example would it be to his son if he chickened out through cowardice?

'How's about it, old son?' he said, chucking Finlay under the chin. 'Can I rely on you to back me up if she starts trying to change the subject?'

If raspberries meant *you bet, Dad*, then he was onto a winner, he decided, as he trailed upstairs with his son to give him a bath and read him his bedtime story.

* * *

Casey needed to get Aaron away from the prying eyes of the Receptionist, not to mention the queue of paying customers the woman at the desk had allowed to pile up because she'd been so busy eavesdropping.

'Is there somewhere private we can go?' she asked him.

'There's the cafe upstairs,' he said.

'Then lead the way.'

They found a quiet alcove, away from the main body of the cafe. Casey waited for Aaron to settle his long, muscular limbs in his seat, thinking to herself that even with the six-pack, bicep, quad and gluts combo he had going for him, she didn't find him the least bit sexy.

What did that say about her, she wondered, that she preferred a man less perfectly formed? Hopefully that she prized brains over brawn. Though more probably that she knew her days of attracting young, buff males were well and truly over — if, in fact, they'd ever existed.

'Okay,' she said. 'Talk to me.'

'It's all a bit embarrassing.' Aaron gripped the table, staring at his hands.

'How about if I grab us a coffee?'

In her experience, a cup of something hot was a great lubricant when, as now, communication had stalled. Aaron threw her a look of gratitude as Casey slipped out of her seat. On her return he seemed more together, she thought, as if he'd been giving himself a good talking-to.

'I was talking to Annie, earlier,' he began.

'I saw her leave,' Casey said. 'She seemed rather ticked-off.'

Aaron's colour rose slightly as he stammered out his words. 'That was me. I upset her really badly, I think.'

'I'm sorry.'

He seemed to take reassurance from her comment. 'I think she's got it into her head that — well, that I was the one who planted all that stuff in her trainers,' he continued. 'That they were presents — love tokens, she called them — from me.'

'And I take it they weren't?'

'Of course not!'

She'd loaded her question with a sympathy she wasn't sure she could afford to feel just yet. Did he know that by blurting all this out he'd just implicated himself? He could be double bluffing, of course — in which case she retracted the stereotypical assumption she'd just made that you couldn't have brains as well as brawn.

There was another puzzle too that needed more light shining on it. What did he mean by *all that stuff*? As far as she knew the amber pendant had been the extent of Annie's ill-gotten gains.

'I've never given Annie so much as a Christmas card before, let alone a present!' He reached for his coffee and cradled it in two hands. It seemed to calm him down. 'Only I didn't handle it too well. Said she was mad, or words to that effect. Probably lots of other stuff too, but

I've forgotten most of it.'

'In your defence she did rather put you on the spot,' Casey said.

Aaron gave her a grateful smile.

'I'm a bit puzzled, though. You said *all that stuff*, as if the pendant wasn't the only thing she claimed to find in her trainer.'

'Well, she said it wasn't. She had other bits of jewellery in her locker. She showed me them. A watch, some earrings, I think, and a bracelet.'

Casey sipped her coffee and digested this information. Once she got back to the station she'd be having a word with the boys in blue who'd conducted the house search at Annie Kovac's and asking them to explain just why it hadn't entered their pretty little heads to search her locker too.

How stupid did this omission make them look! Now Annie had got away with even more swag. Walked right past her at Reception with it sitting in her handbag not half an hour ago. Casey wasn't a blusher. But she felt deeply humiliated.

Thankfully, Aaron Strummer was so

wrapped up in his contretemps with Annie that he uttered not one word about police incompetence. If he had, she'd have been forced to sit here and take it on the chin because really there was no excuse for such a cock-up. There was a modicum of relief to be got from the fact that he was clearly a couple of steps behind her.

'How do I know you're telling me the truth, Aaron?' she said. 'For all I know Annie's right and you *did* put those things in her shoe.'

Aaron stared at her, completely taken aback by the sudden turn of events.

'Maybe you never meant them as love tokens. But what if you planted them there, just to get her into trouble?'

'That's ridiculous!' An irate Aaron slammed his fist on the table hard. Coffee leapt from his cup and spilled over the side. 'I'm no house-breaker and neither is Annie. And why would what I want to get Annie into trouble anyway? I like her.'

He looked away, embarrassed. So she was right in her earlier assumption that Aaron had feelings for Annie. He was suffering because he'd humiliated her earlier and now he longed for the chance to put it right.

'You think she's innocent, don't you?'

'Like I said. Annie's solid, through and through.'

'But she's not so convinced about you, is she? Seems to me she's suspected you all along. And it's because she wants to protect you that she's meekly allowed herself to be arrested for a crime she thought you'd committed.'

The penny suddenly seemed to drop. Finally. There was no guile in this young man's make-up, Casey was convinced. He hadn't seen this coming. But did lack of guile necessarily mean innocence? It could equally signify stupidity.

Casey reeled off the dates and approximate times of all four house break-ins for which Annie was implicated.

'Do *you* have alibis for those times, Aaron?' she asked.

'Alibis? Me?' He blinked. 'I was probably here. I'm always here. Look, tell me those dates and times again.'

Casey scrabbled in her bag for a pen,

reached for a paper napkin and wrote them down.

'Yes. Definitely I was here,' he said, squinting at the dates that the napkin was already soaking up. 'Check with my manager. And while we're at it, all those times you've got down there are times when Annie's classes are on too.' He raised his eyes and fixed her with an aggrieved stare. 'Didn't you check her alibis?'

It was to his credit that he was just as concerned with letting Annie off the hook as he was about defending himself, Casey mused, as she considered his question. She sincerely hoped that Annie's alibis had been checked with a fine-toothed comb. But given that she'd just discovered how half-hearted the search on her property had been, she wasn't going to swear to it.

But she couldn't think about that just now — not while something else was demanding her attention. What had started as a small itch was now shouting to be scratched. A sudden image of Thea Mitchell's trainers by the door had lodged itself in her brain — the first things Casey had seen when she'd gone to take Thea's statement. Back then they'd stuck in her mind because they'd acted as a timely reminder to get her act together and book a few classes down at the Fitness Centre. But now they were stuck in her head for a different reason altogether.

Thea Mitchell was a regular at Annie's classes. Charlotte Grainger, another victim, was one more. It was by sheer chance that the officer sent to Charlotte Grainger's house to take her statement was Gail. Had it been anyone else — herself included — there could have been no guarantee that her whereabouts on the night of the break-in would ever have come to light.

It was only because Gail and Charlotte — though not exactly friends — had seen each other often enough at Annie's aerobics class to recognise each other as class mates that this bit of knowledge came to light. So, what if the two other victims took Annie's classes too? There was one way to find out — by ringing them.

Annie Kovac taught most mornings,

afternoons and evenings if Aaron Strummer were to be believed. It would take a matter of minutes to check her timetable with the Manager, even if she didn't believe what he'd just told her. Was it possible that whoever had broken into these women's houses had inside knowledge about when the occupants would be out?

Something Thea Mitchell said came back to her:- *Do you think they were watching the house? Waiting for me to go out so they could rob me?* Casey had replied she thought it unlikely and said it was more probably an opportunistic crime. But now she wasn't so sure.

She should stop putting the wind up poor Aaron Strummer right now. Poor lad had enough on his plate already worrying about how badly he'd offended Annie. It certainly said something about his feelings for her if he were willing to ignore the fact that in the eyes of her Manager she was a criminal. She guessed it wouldn't have mattered to him if Annie had been decked out like a jeweller's front window. She was one hundred per cent innocent as far as he was concerned. He was probably right too.

'Look, Aaron,' she said, 'I have a couple of calls to make. Why don't you make one yourself? To Annie. She needs a friend right now, wouldn't you say?'

'Have you finished with me, then?' he said, looking relieved.

'Done and dusted. You've been most helpful.'

'You're not really convinced Annie had anything to do with those robberies are you, Inspector?'

She'd seriously underestimated Aaron Strummer, she realised. There was far more about him than a perfect body. He was a young man with excellent instincts.

'Give her a ring,' she said. 'Tell her it won't be long before we drop the charges.'

It delighted her to see how his face turned pink with pleasure. Oh to be young and in love, she thought as she made her way out of the cafe. Speaking of romance, she thought, she really ought to go home, which was where she'd been heading before Gail persuaded her she might feel better after a workout. How many hours ago was that?

Dom had been understanding when she rang to tell him she'd run into a bit of trouble at the Sports Centre and she was going to have to hang around until it got cleared up. But she doubted he'd appreciate it if her devotion to duty led her back to the station to check the statements of the two other women who'd been burgled, just to see if there was any mention of where they'd been when the break-ins had occurred.

It would have to wait until tomorrow.

⋆ ⋆ ⋆

Casey woke up firing on all cylinders, desperate to get to work. There was just so much to be done. But she wasn't so wrapped up in herself to spot that something wasn't quite right with Dom. It wasn't like him to be so quiet.

'Are you ill?' she asked him, as she knelt to fasten her trainers. A power walk this morning, she'd already decided. She had far too much nervous energy pumping round her body to ride the bike.

'Me? No.' He looked at her dreamily.

'Have I done something then?' It was always a possibility. She racked her brains. 'Did I take the last banana again?'

He grinned at her. 'You always take the last banana,' he said. 'And since you've been on this health kick the last apple and the last orange too.'

Casey pulled a face. 'I'll get some more,' she promised. 'I'm off this afternoon.'

Dom's face brightened. 'So you'll be home early,' he said.

'I thought I might go for a swim first.'

'Oh.' The silence between them was growing heavier. Now she was certain she'd done something.

'I'll come straight back if you like,' she offered.

'It would be nice. We haven't spent much time together lately,' Dom said. 'We could have lunch. A slimline lunch, of course,' he hastily added, at the sight of Casey's startled expression. 'It'd be a chance to talk.'

'What about?' She didn't like the sound

of this. When Dom suggested talking it was usually about the precarious state of their finances or renovating the house, neither of which appealed much to her as topics of conversation. Suddenly that swim seemed an even better idea.

'I'll ring you,' she said, planting an affectionate kiss on his cheek, 'and let you know when to expect me.'

What's got into him, she wondered, as she sprinted off down the path.

* * *

Once at her desk, however, all thoughts of lunch with Dom, slimline or otherwise, went right out of her head. She needed to get her hands on those statements.

It was exactly as she'd thought. Both women had left their houses empty but neither had said where they'd been. The very first break-in had occurred about five weeks ago, now, some time on a Wednesday between the hours of nine in the morning and four in the afternoon at the house of a Mrs Jenny Cadman. The second less than a week later during the hours of two and four, this time on a Thursday.

Casey reached for her phone and dialled Jenny Cadman's number. Typically, all she got was a recorded message. Casey left her details, asking Mrs Cadman to ring her at her earliest convenience.

She was luckier with her next caller, a Margaret Enright.

'Have you traced my stuff?' was the first thing she said as soon as Casey introduced herself.

Casey didn't enjoy admitting that so far no, they hadn't.

'Oh.'

Margaret Enright's initial friendliness quickly evaporated. She was beginning to sound aggrieved. Casey decided to cut to the chase, before the woman started taking a pop at her.

'Mrs Enright, I wonder — can you remember where you were on the day of the break-in?'

In the silence between her question and the reply, Casey's phone gave a ping, closely followed by another, to signal that she'd just received two messages in quick succession. Hopefully one was from Jenny Cadman, returning her call.

'Yes. It was Wednesday, wasn't it? So it's a no brainer,' Mrs Enright said. 'I was working from home till two, as usual, then I drove over to the Sports Centre. I have an aerobics class that runs between two thirty and three thirty.'

Casey's heart gave a little leap.

'With someone called Annie Kovac?'

'That's right. Annie. Pity she didn't take this week's class. Some sub did it. Nowhere near as good as Annie. I did ask at Reception when she'd be back but I didn't get a straight answer. There's something fishy going on there, if you ask me. If Annie's left then there'll be loads of women following her to find out where she's teaching now. Aerobics teachers are like hairdressers, aren't they?'

'Excuse me?' Casey could have kicked herself for asking for an explanation. She really wanted to get off the phone and pick up her other messages.

'You know. When you get a good one you'd be mad to let them go.'

Ah, she got it now. Quickly, she thanked Mrs Enright for her co-operation, assured her the case was a priority and hung up. Checking her messages she saw she was right. Jenny Cadman had got back to her. The other message was from Soco. Goodness, she'd forgotten all about ringing them back. Deciding that it must be urgent for them to ring her again so soon, she quickly called her voicemail.

What she heard made her jump two feet in the air. Scene of crime officers had found a key under the kebab van belonging to Nico Demetriades. The key was attached to a brick-red rubber band two centimetres thick and the number 141 was printed on it. It looked like a locker key, the person who'd left the message said.

Oh, it did that all right, Casey thought. And more. Brick red was the colour of all the rubber bands attached to all the locker keys at the Fitness Centre. Was it a coincidence or were the break-ins and the attack on Nico Demetriades somehow connected?

Well, she wouldn't discover the answer

to that sitting at her desk. She needed to go over there immediately and check if the key to locker 141 was missing. But first she needed to listen to her other message.

Jenny Cadman had been at an aerobics class the afternoon her house was burgled, she discovered when she played back the voice mail. She didn't say with whom, but she didn't need to. Casey had committed the sports centre time table to memory. The only aerobics class taking place at that time and on that day was led by Annie Kovac.

Immediately she called Soco. This time she got through to the very officer who'd left her message. Once she'd explained her suspicions about where the key had originally come from, between them they made an arrangement to meet down at the centre within the next thirty minutes.

'I'm off out if anybody wants me,' Casey said to the room in general, ignoring the usual grumbles of *skiving again* and *part-timer*, that followed in her wake.

A sudden thought flashed up. There were four changing rooms down at the centre, two dry, two wet, male and female. She had no qualms about going into the female changing rooms to try the key. But she baulked at going into the men's. All that naked male flesh in close up. No thanks.

'Are you busy right now?' She beamed at the young P.C. loitering by the door. Perhaps imagining he'd been singled out for glory, he turned pink and beamed back. 'Only I could do with a bit of help. I'll fill you in on the way.'

* * *

The Receptionist had caused a bit of a rumpus when Casey flashed her I.D. and informed her they were here to conduct a search. *Didn't they need a warrant to do that*, she demanded, pink in the face. Assuring her that they didn't, they left the poor woman floundering in their wake as they passed on, leaving the young P.C. to stand guard at Reception, with instructions to let no one in or out for the moment.

The dry changing rooms through the

double doors revealed only that the lockers were numbered one to fifty in the men's changing rooms and fifty one to a hundred in the women's. Casey almost ran the length of the corridor to get to the dry changing rooms, the Soco officer, John Smailes, hot on her heels.

Ducking her head round the door of the female changing room revealed immediately that the locker numbers went from one hundred and fifty one to two hundred.

John Smaile's excited yell sent her scurrying next door, all her previous concerns of naked male bodies completely forgotten.

'You've got 141?' She almost tripped over a pair of trainers in her hurry. John already had the key out. She hovered behind him, her blood pumping in her ears.

'Come on, come on!' she hissed.

'Damn thing's stuck.'

She elbowed him aside. 'Let me do it,' she said. 'I know how these locker keys work. They're awkward beggars. There!'

The door fell open.

'Don't touch anything!' John yelled, as

he fished from his bag a pair of latex gloves and struggled to put them on.

He rummaged around for a bit before he dragged out a man's tracksuit.

'Bit whiffy.' He wrinkled his nose, trying all the pockets. 'Just in case he's left his name and address,' he joked.

'Now that would be helpful,' Casey said.

John Smailes' face suddenly lit up. 'Well, well, well,' he said. 'What have we got here, then! Feast your eyes on these little beauties, Casey.'

Casey didn't know what she'd been expecting. A couple of pellets from the air gun used in the attack on Mr Demetriades, perhaps. She'd have been happy enough with that. But a pair of sparkling diamond earrings? That *was* a surprise.

* * *

Casey admired the methodical manner in which John Smailes approached the task of bagging the items they'd discovered in the locker, and the neatness of his handwriting on the labels he attached.

Had it been up to her she'd probably have dropped the tracksuit on the floor in her excitement, thereby contaminating the evidence. There was every likelihood too she'd have lost one of the earrings down the back of the lockers.

'So, where do we go from here?' Smailes wanted to know.

'Well, it's a puzzle. I thought we might discover some evidence that might help us find out who attacked Nico Demetriades and attempted to steal his takings,' Casey said. 'But this puts things in a whole new light.'

Smailes agreed. 'Maybe we could convince ourselves it was a coincidence, coming across a locker key that belonged to this particular centre. But finding those diamond earrings and knowing what we know about the house break-ins. Well, there's got to be a connection, hasn't there?'

'Certainly looks like it. We'll know more once the earrings have been identified of course.' A quick phone call to the station would reveal the name of the woman from whom they'd been taken, then all they needed to do would be to ask her to step into the station to identify them as hers.

'Who has access to the centre's client list? You know, names, addresses, all that stuff?' Smailes asked her. 'You said, didn't you, that all these victims were female and all are members?'

Casey nodded. 'That's right.' She was thinking hard. The obvious person to have access to clients' details was the Receptionist, Terri Gregson. But she only worked office hours and the centre was open from seven in the morning till ten at night and at weekends. When she wasn't there, anybody would jump in who wasn't otherwise engaged coaching, or manning the pool or gym, as she'd witnessed herself many times on her way in and out.

There were at least dozen members of staff who worked at the centre and all of them were going to have to be interviewed, which meant bringing in all those currently off-duty or, as in Annie Kovac's case, suspended. Casey still thought she was innocent, but a court of law might not see it like that, in light of the fact that she'd been caught with a whopping amber pendant that belonged to another woman round her neck.

'We're going to have to interview everyone who works here who has the centre's computer password,' she said, glumly.

The clock in the changing room said twelve twelve. She should have clocked off twelve minutes ago. Maybe she should just give Dom a quick ring. Tell him she'd have to miss their lunch. He was bound to understand.

Normally she'd have happily convinced herself this was the case. But today she couldn't help feeling uneasy. There was something not quite right with Dom. She hadn't been able to put her finger on it this morning, but she knew him. He was holding back about something. All this *it'd be nice to have lunch* rubbish. It was code for something else, she was convinced.

Her stomach took a sudden dive. What if he were ill? Really ill, she meant, with some dreadful disease from which he would never recover and he was about to break the news? And here she was, putting him off, just because of a case. Like she was the only Inspector in the entire service of Brockhaven CID who knew how to conduct an interview!

Something Margaret Enright had said to her over the phone suddenly leapt into her head. Fair enough, she'd been talking about aerobics instructors and hairdressers at the time. *When you get a good one you'd be mad to let them go*. But didn't this apply to men too?

'Casey, are you all right?'

John Smailes was looking at her strangely.

'I'm just wondering who to call to conduct these interviews. We'll need a couple of officers at least,' she said. 'Unfortunately I can't be here to do them myself.'

'Got something more urgent to deal with, is it?' he said, his tone full of understanding.

'That's right, John,' she said. 'And I should have left fifteen minutes ago.'

* * *

There was no sign of lunch or of Dom either when she got home. Casey wandered from room to room, calling his name to no avail. Typical! She'd rushed all the way back — completely forgetting to call in at the shops for the fruit she'd promised to replace in her eagerness — and he wasn't even here.

Then she remembered the awful thought she'd had back in the changing room at the Fitness centre — of Dom in the early stages of terminal decline, and she felt suddenly guilty. It occurred to her he may be feeling unwell and have taken to his bed. In a flash she was at the top of the stairs, flinging open the door to their bedroom.

'Dom!'

The room was empty. It was all very peculiar. She wandered over to the window and looked out onto the empty street. Empty, that was, apart from Dom's battered old VW. Her earlier anxiety completely evaporated as it came chugging round the corner into the street and pulled up outside the house.

She watched him get out, stroll round to the back, open the boot and take out a number of shopping bags. One glance informed her that Dom hadn't visited their usual emporium but had gone vastly upmarket. And wasn't that a bottle of champagne poking out of one bag? What on earth was going on?

Taking the steps two at a time she reached the front door and opened it before he got there. Casey wouldn't have said he looked disappointed to see her, but he certainly looked *something. Caught in the act*, she would have said. *Up to no good. Shifty*.

'Pushing the boat out, aren't we?' She eyed the bags suspiciously, making no attempt to help him with them. 'Were you expecting somebody special?'

Another woman, for instance? No, that was ludicrous. Now he was grinning like a gormless idiot. One of those bags had those special biscuits she liked in it, and all manner of fancy cheeses to go with them. And olives! They never had olives unless they were affixed to a frozen pizza, these days.

'You, you idiot! Didn't I tell you I was making lunch? Only I didn't expect you to get here on time, did I? You never usually do.'

Back and forth he trailed picking up bags and plonking them onto the kitchen work surface. In the end she decided she might as well give him a hand and picked up the last two with studied nonchalance.

'So, what are we celebrating?'

Lunch, when Dom did it, usually consisted of something on toast. This was a spread worthy of a toff's picnic. Dom closed the freezer, into which he'd just popped the bottle of champagne, turned round and leaned against it, arms crossed. His expression had changed — it was deadly serious now.

'I don't know if we are,' he said. 'It really depends on you. I want to ask you something.'

Alarm bells suddenly started ringing somewhere inside Casey's head. Suddenly she knew exactly what was coming. You didn't buy champagne to announce your demise. She slumped down into the nearest chair and waited.

'But first I want you to turn your phone off.'

Casey fumbled for the mobile that in her job was a third hand, and switched it off. She wondered why she'd put up no resistance. Curiosity about what came next wasn't really a good enough reason. Because deep down she already knew what was coming next. She could have told him to hold it right there. But it was as if an invisible bird had suddenly swooped down from the sky and tugged out her tongue.

'Do you know when I first fell in love with you, Casey Clunes?'

She shook her head.

'You were snooping round my old house, remember? In the tea chests?'

Snooping? What did he mean snooping? Dom had inherited his parents' bungalow. Most of their stuff he'd packed away. She'd discovered an exquisite china tea service and berated him for not using it. He was afraid of chipping the cups or breaking the saucers, he said, which is why he only ever brought them out on special occasions, preferring to use cheap mugs for every day.

'What's the point, you said, of keeping

things for best? Life is for living, not wrapping up and storing in the dark. Who cares if you break a few saucers on the way!'

Had she really said that? And he'd remembered all this time. That tea service really had been lovely. Shame they only had half a dozen pieces still intact. And extremely decent of Dom not to bring that fact up.

'Will you marry me, Casey Clunes?' Dom said.

The bird was back. This time with an accompanying flock of mates, who between them were in the process of removing all her bones. She'd suddenly gone all wobbly. Dom's face, lit up with love, suddenly struck her as being the most perfect face of anybody she'd ever known. She could have put up a fight. It was her usual way, after all. But she didn't. Instead she just came out with it. Yes.

'I never expected it to be so easy,' Dom said. He looked as if he were about to explode with delight.

'Funny that,' Casey said. 'Neither did I.'

But she had no intentions of changing

her mind. She'd never been that kind of girl.

* * *

It wasn't every day you got engaged. So in the excitement of the champagne-fuelled lunch, which led to the continuation of the celebration upstairs — thankfully made possible by the fact that Dom had earlier persuaded Debbie the nanny to take Finlay out for the whole day — and then the two hour nap that followed, it was hardly surprising that Casey forgot to turn her phone back on till next morning.

When she finally did, two messages jumped out at her, putting all other thought in the shade. Both were from Jenny Cadman.

'Can you please ring me back as soon as you get this?'

The time of the first call was 5 o'clock the previous afternoon. The second had come three hours later and said much the same thing. It was now eight fifteen in the morning.

'I have to go,' she yelled up to Dom

from the bottom of the stairs. He was in the bathroom, singing along to the radio. 'And answer came there none,' she added with a smile, popping back into the kitchen to drop a farewell kiss on Finlay's head.

'Will you be Mrs Talbot when you get married?' Debbie was supervising Finlay eating breakfast in his high chair. Finlay clapped his hands gleefully when he spotted Casey, his eyes as wide as saucers.

Debbie had been so excited when she'd spotted the diamond ring on Casey's finger that she'd been in danger of hyperventilating, Casey thought. It had immediately occurred to her that Debbie's reaction was just the start of the fuss. Once it got round at work it wouldn't stop. Oh, well, she'd get used to it, she imagined.

'Change my name?' The idea had previously never occurred to Casey. She'd agreed to marry Dom, not to relinquish her own identity. 'We'll have to have a chat about that one, Debbie,' she said. 'But meanwhile, D.I. Casey Clunes has an important house call to make.'

* * *

'Thank goodness. I was just about to come round to the Police Station myself.' Jenny Cadman held the door open wide for Casey. She seemed keyed up, like she'd been doing a lot of thinking and not much sleeping.

Casey apologised for her tardiness. To make amends she wiped her feet extremely carefully before entering the hall, which seemed to go some way to pacifying Ms Cadman.

'There's something I forgot to mention when I called you,' she said. 'It might be important.'

'Shall we go through?'

The living room and dining room had been knocked into one, to give a feeling of elegant spaciousness. It was the abode of a single woman, without a doubt, Casey thought, with a pang of envy. At Casey's instigation, Ms Cadman began her story.

'I had a phone call. From Reception at the Centre. Just a couple of hours before I left for my aerobics class on the afternoon

I was burgled. They wanted to know if I was coming to the class that afternoon.'

Now this was interesting! Casey pricked up her ears. 'Did they give a name? Was it a man or a woman?'

'A male voice, anyway, though I wouldn't swear that it was an adult one. I wasn't in the least suspicious until I remembered it yesterday,' she said. 'But then when I thought about it again, I realised it probably wasn't Reception at all.'

Casey's phone suddenly started ringing. It was John Smailes.

'Do you mind if I get this?' she asked.

'Be my guest.'

John Smailes was brief and to the point. 'Ashley Gregson,' he said. 'His fingerprints were all over those earrings and we found traces of his DNA on the tracksuit.'

Casey racked her brains. 'Do we know him then?' He must have had dealings with the Law before if his details were on record, she reasoned.

'Youth offender. He got a community sentence after several reprimands for antisocial behaviour.'

'Address?'

'Winston Churchill Road. Number ten.'

Well, that was a stroke of luck. Winston Churchill was just a two-minute drive away. Her brain had started to go into overdrive. She'd pretty well memorised the names of all the employees at the centre. There was no Ashley Gregson. But there was a Terri Gregson.

'Thanks, John. You've been very helpful.'

* * *

Ashley Gregson's anti-social tendencies were reflected in the anti-social hours he kept. It took a prolonged assault on the doorbell before he eventually prised his scuzzy head out from under his duvet and showed his pustular visage at the front door where Casey, after taking leave of Jenny Cadman, was waiting for him with another officer, P.C. Jones, who'd been despatched in case of trouble.

Going inside should have been a matter of routine. But that was before an irate

Terri Gregson came charging up the path, litre carton of milk in one hand and sliced white wrapped loaf in another.

'What the hell do you think you're doing?' she squawked. 'Good job I got back from the shop when I did, isn't it!'

Casey, who'd only ever seen Terri Gregson behaving like the consummate professional in her role of Receptionist, was quite taken aback. Oddly, under the circumstances, her harsh manner was directed at Casey and the P.C.

To Ashley, whose skinny white legs in boxers protruded from a dirty white T-shirt, bearing the legend, Rock My World and who'd sleep-walked downstairs to the front door, she simply said, 'It's all right, Ash. I'll deal with these people.'

They followed her inside, ignoring her assertion that they needed a warrant. They didn't, Casey said. Not when they had Ashley's prints all over a pair of diamond earrings they'd found in a locker back at the Fitness Centre, in the pocket of a tracksuit that had so much of his DNA over it they could clone him from it.

Terri shot her son a look of fury. He returned it with a glare.

'Godssake, Ash,' she snapped. 'Why didn't you get rid of that tracksuit like I told you to?'

The boy shrugged, scratched his groin and muttered something incomprehensible in teenage-boy speak.

'Mrs Gregson,' Casey said, 'am I right in assuming that you were already aware your son was involved in a brutal attack on a Mr Demetriades who runs the kebab van in the market square?'

'He didn't shoot that air rifle,' she replied, as if that excused him. 'Nor carry the knife. My Ashley's not like that.'

She'd read the news reports then. A doting mother, obviously. Casey was familiar with the type.

'Led astray was he, Mrs Gregson?' P.C. Jones put in. 'By the bigger boys?'

Terri Gregson pursed her lip-glossed lips.

'And what about the break-ins?' Casey reminded the Gregsons about the earrings they'd found. They'd be conducting a full search of the house when their colleagues arrived.

'Well, you won't find much.' Ashley spoke the first coherent words he'd said yet.

'Is that so?' Casey turned her attention back to his mother. 'Is that because you've been drip feeding the stolen goods in another direction? Depositing them in Annie Kovac's trainers, for example? Is that where those diamond earrings were heading?'

Terri Gregson had the grace to look ashamed.

'Shame Annie was suspended before you could plant another load of stuff on her.'

'I had to help my son, didn't I? He's already been in trouble with the law. But he's eighteen now. He can't afford to mess up again.'

She'd made a deal with him, she said, when she'd found jewellery under his bed. He'd confessed about the break-ins but had suddenly got cold feet about selling on the stuff. He was bright enough to realise that the Police would have informed local jewellers to keep an eye out for it. They made a deal. If he promised to stop immediately she'd help him get rid of the stuff.

'So what had Annie Kovac ever done to you that you felt you needed to implicate her in not just one but four burglaries?' Casey said.

'Oh, do me a favour. Have you seen her? The way she looks? The way they all fall over themselves whenever she walks in?'

Jealousy, then. Pure and simple.

She'd given him a locker key and told him to hide everything he'd taken inside the locker. She couldn't risk the Police finding it on her property, she'd told him. But then, like the idiot he was, he'd gone and got involved with his old mates again, helping them with their dirty work. And he'd dropped the wretched key near Mr Demetriades' van.

'We'll have the names of the mates, please,' Casey said. 'And then you can come down to the station. Both of you,' she added, in case Terri Gregson harboured any funny ideas that she was innocent.

* * *

Casey and Dom were celebrating. They were sitting in the back of a taxi en route to The Blue Delphinium, a couple of miles out of Brockhaven on the coast road.

Casey was happy, relaxed and excited all rolled into one. Relaxed because she'd solved two cases for the price of one, and because earlier that day she'd had a phone call from Nico Demetriades, thanking her for her hard work and offering her free kebabs for as long as she remained in Brockhaven. Happy because Annie Kovac had been reinstated and because when she'd tried on her little black dress earlier in the evening it fitted like a glove. And excited because she'd never eaten at a Michelin starred restaurant before. The evening stretched before her, promising magic.

Half an hour later, they were back in the same taxi, heading back to Brockhaven.

'How was I to know the Maitre D' was serious when he said 2012? I thought he meant 2011.'

Dom was clearly mortified. When he'd phoned the restaurant he'd asked for a table for the fifth of September, which had been a week away at the time. He'd been given the date all right. But for the following year.

'Honestly, Dom, I don't mind. Anybody would have thought the same thing. It's not as if we're never going to sample the cuisine there, is it?' She squeezed his hand reassuringly.

'I should have realised there was a year long waiting list.'

Casey's mouth twitched. 'You've got to see the funny side, Dom,' she said.

The taxi had reached the outskirts of Brockhaven. They had to decide whether to go home or stay in town. Remembering they'd paid for a babysitter they got the taxi driver to drop them off in the market place.

'Mmm! I smell kebabs!' Dom was quite cheered up now he knew Casey wasn't just play-acting and really didn't bear a grudge.

'Look! Mr Demetriades is back!'

Joining the queue for kebabs was a

no-brainer. When their turn arrived Mr Demetriades beamed at Casey.

'Come to claim your first free kebab?' he beamed. 'I see you've brought a friend.'

'This is Dom, Mr Demetriades.' She decided to come clean. She didn't want him to think she was taking advantage of his generous offer. 'Actually, we were on our way to a restaurant to celebrate our engagement but there was a bit of a mix up about dates so we came home.'

Mr Demetriades wiped his hands on a nearby towel and beamed at Dom.

'Engaged! Let me shake you by the hands, Mr Casey. You're a very lucky man!'

He pumped Dom's arm up and down vigorously for several seconds before releasing it, insisting they were both to have anything they wanted as well as all the trimmings. Dom, who was not by nature effusive, endured the hand pumping, good naturedly, though the grin fixed to his face betrayed exactly how much he wished he was anywhere but here.

Fortunately, just as he'd finished serving them, a crowd turned up and Mr Demetriades suddenly got very busy, which allowed them to slip away. They munched their stuffed pittas, dripping grease and sauce down their chins in heavenly, companiable silence, making their way down the high street, heading for the sea front in unspoken agreement.

Just ahead of them, on the other side of the street, Casey thought she recognised the tall, athletic figure of Aaron Strummer at the bus stop. She pointed him out to Dom.

'Better not let him see you eating this kebab,' Dom teased. 'It'll be cross-trainers at dawn.'

'You're right,' she said. 'We'll wait here till he's gone.'

They didn't have to wait long. When the bus pulled up, disgorging passengers, Annie Kovac was among them. She stepped into Aaron's arms and shyly kissed his cheek.

'Aaw.' Casey was touched. That was one more thing to be happy and relieved about. The boy had seen sense at last.

'Love's young dream.'

Dom, who'd missed all this, so intently had he been gazing at his fiancée's face, wiped an endearing smear of hot sauce from the tip of Casey's nose.

'Yes,' he said. 'I guess we are, aren't we? Now, why don't you come over here and give me a big kiss.'

THE END